4

PETER
BUCKLEY

FIELDS
OF
BLOOD

Fields of Blood

By

Peter Buckley

Contents

Page

1

The photocopied flyers had been handed out to students in the week building up to Halloween. Truman High School students that had been given a flyer had secretly whispered about the party in classrooms when the teachers weren't present. The moment they had walked into class or back into earshot, all conversation ceased. In a small town like Truman, Pennsylvania everyone knew everyone else's business and what was going on. The high school students wanted the Halloween party to be just for them, without the fear of the adults of the town stopping their fun. Over the years, the farms and farmland that surround the town and its population of 4,608 had struggled with the advancement of technology, and only a handful still produced and sold their crops and cattle for a small living profit. A group of students from the school had found an old derelict barn on the outskirts of town. The farm it had belonged too had been deserted for some time. The fields surrounding it had been bought by another farm owner some miles down the road, and wheat and corn fields surrounded the old, rotten, wooden buildings. They had begun to take bits of equipment and decorations to the barn for the last week. Music would be provided by a battery-powered sound system that could be plugged into one of the teenager's phones that stored music. Kegs of beer had been stolen from delivery trucks or acquired by the older students using fake identification from liquor stores in neighboring towns.

The plan was simple. Get all dressed up and head out as usual as darkness descended to walk the streets during Halloween night where youngsters trick or treated, head over to the barn, party until midnight and then head back. Parents were used to kids playing pranks and hanging out till the early hours on Halloween, especially as it was a Friday night. The local sheriff and his deputies casually patrolled the streets, knowing that the moment they were seen that the groups of youngsters would run and hide, but nothing bad ever happened. There was the occasional egg on a window, burning dog crap left on doorsteps, or toilet paper thrown into trees or over buildings—nothing that couldn't be cleaned up.

Paula and Toby had been dating for the past six months. It was a very innocent relationship. While most seventeen year olds were experimenting and enjoying the investigation of each other's bodies, they were both churchgoing kids. They had met at church, where their parents attended every Sunday. Their parents encouraged them to begin dating, both sets of parents knowing each other and preferring to have some form of control over who their son and daughter dated. Paula had been handed the black and white flyer and had taken it to Toby. She was becoming tired of her ritualistic life of: get up, help with breakfast for her father and brothers, go to school, go home, do homework, and do chores. There was even a time limit on the phone when speaking to Toby. She could only see Toby on Tuesday and Thursday evenings, where they were only allowed downstairs and not allowed to go up to her room. Her parents wanted to make sure nothing unhealthy happened between them. She had craved something different—a little adventure in her life. The Halloween party was it. She had always gone out into the community with the others kids, so she knew she would be allowed to go out with all the others, although dressing up as some unholy beast or ghoul was frowned upon, so she never dressed up. This Halloween was going to be different. She had already begun hiding parts of a vampire costume she had been making.

Toby was reluctant at first to go to the barn on Halloween. He too had never taken part in the dressing up part of the evening. His parents had also not wanted their son to begin to act out some murderous fiend. They had always allowed him to go out with the others, and in the past, he had trick or treated, feeling stupid that while others had run up to doors and collected candy from the different houses, getting words of praise for their costumes, he stood there in his jeans and shirt.

Paula had pestered him for days about the party. He had finally given in and agreed but wasn't going to dress up. If his parents found any form of costume, he didn't want to face trying to explain it to his teary mother. She would burst into tears and tell him that he had disappointed her and broken her heart whenever he did something wrong or had not achieved well enough in school.

Others had spent weeks getting their costumes ready. The party at the barn was going to be the party of the century. If there was a way of capturing the excitement and nervous energy that flowed around the school and from between the different groups of friends that had been invited, it would have lit the town for a week. Locals had noticed the difference: the younger generation were happier, polite and eager to help.

Some of Paula and Toby's classmates had found an old Ouija board game in one of their basements and had taken it over to the barn. They had talked at length about using it at midnight. A couple of them had looked into the town's past to try and find the best place to use it, hoping that if they could find a place where death had occurred then they could try and contact that deceased person through the Ouija board.

James and Frank had taken it on themselves to investigate the best place to go with the board and had found that the very farm they were going to have the party was part of an area where during the American civil war hundreds had been killed in a skirmish between the two sides. There was no mention or evidence to say where those that had died were buried. Frank suggested that those who had been killed would have been buried at the cemetery.

They also found a small newspaper article about a young woman who had been found hanging from a tree in one of the fields. The article stated that suicide was the cause of death. Further down the page was a small piece,

13

highlighting the unknown whereabouts of an eighteen year old male who had been missing for six days.

2

Halloween arrived. School had ended, and every student vacated the premises quicker than normal. As darkness fell, the trick or treaters headed out onto the streets. The youngsters walked the streets with guardians or parents, who guided them from house to house, remaining on the sidewalk as the youngsters skipped their way down the various pathways and up to the doors and either rang the bells or knocked excitedly. The waiting adult escorts waved at the homeowners as they handed out candy to the children.

The older kids of the community roamed around, jumping out on unsuspecting passers-by, they took it in turns to try and frighten each other. Some buried themselves in the piles of dead leaves that had been gathered up on the grass verges. Others jumped up out of garbage cans. Some even went as far as climbing trees and dropping out of them onto friends below.

Paula had told her mother and father that she was going out with a group of her friends to trick or treat and that Toby was going with her. Her mother had looked her up and down, seeing if she could see any signs of costume or excessive makeup. Satisfied, Paula's mother nodded her permission. Toby arrived and rang the doorbell, Paula couldn't get out quick enough, shouting 'See you later' as she closed the door. She dragged Toby down the path and down the sidewalk to where she knew her mother couldn't see her. Paula watched from her vantage point, waiting for her mother's shadow that stood at the window blinds to disappear before sneaking back for the bag and costume she had thrown out of her bedroom window earlier. Toby waited, nervously shaking his head.

They walked hand in hand until they reached the end of the tree-lined street, where an old empty house sat. It had been empty for some time. It was surrounded by a large white wall. The gate had been broken and swung loosely on one hinge. The house had already been the target of the egg-wielding youngsters, seeing it as a haunted house because it was empty and dark. Toilet paper had also been launched into the front garden and hung like streamers from the lonesome tree that stood in the center of the overgrown, grassy front yard. Paula pulled Toby in past the gate and below the tree. A street lamp directly outside the house shone brightly, and a small amount of light broke through the bare branches of the tree down onto the two. Paula dropped the bag on the floor and unzipped it. She pulled out a long black dress and rested it on a nearby branch. Toby looked around nervously as his girlfriend began to undress.

'What are you doing?' he asked, shocked by what he was witnessing.

'I'm going to get changed into my costume,' she answered.

The cold October air attacked her flesh, and goose pimples immediately sprang to life, yet she didn't feel the cold. The excitement kept her warm, or at least kept her mind off the coldness.

Toby stood staring at her. It was the first time he had seen her in nothing but bra and panties. She looked at him. Seeing the excitement in his face, she ran her right forefinger under the left shoulder strap of her bra, slid it off her shoulder and gently pulled her bra down far enough to expose her erect nipple. Toby could feel his heart begin to pound. His stomach felt like it was full of flapping birds. He began to shiver, not from the cold but from the sudden hormonal surge.

Paula gentle squeezed her nipple before moving closer to Toby and kissing him passionately. He found his hand reaching up and cupping her naked breast. A gentle moan escaped his girlfriend's mouth as they kissed. He could feel heat and pain emanating from his groin as his manhood struggled against the resistance of his jeans.

She pulled away from him. Her eyes were closed, but her expression was one of excitement. He kissed her neck and then slowly moved down until he finally found he erect nipple. He teased it with his tongue and then wrapped his mouth over it and gently sucked. She moaned louder as the pleasure ran through her body. Toby moved back up away from her nipple and kissed the flesh of her breast and then began to suck a little harder. Paula could feel him sucking and smiled. She wanted more but then suddenly realized that this wasn't the right time or place.

Paula then pushed him away. 'I think tonight is going to be an exciting night,' she said.

She quickly pulled her bra up and wriggled into the long, slim-fitting dress.

'Oh shit,' Toby said.

'What?' Paula asked, concerned.

Toby put a hand over his face and shook his head. 'I'm sorry, I got carried away.'

Paula looked down and saw the dark mark left by Toby's sucking on her breast.

'Oh my, I just hope I my mum doesn't see it, otherwise we are both in deep trouble.'

Toby stood, his emotions in tatters. He breathed heavily and found himself placing his hands in his jean pockets to try and mask the bulge that had grown there.

He finally understood what the excitement was all about. He had listened to others in the gym locker room boast and share their fumbling sexual experiences and had wondered why they got so childish and silly. Now he knew why.

Paula pulled out a small makeup mirror from her bag and applied some black lipstick she had borrowed from one her friends. She strained her eyes in the low, shadow-filled light below the tree, making sure it was even. She placed her other clothes into the bag and then together they returned to the sidewalk.

They walked down the street until they finally met up with some of the others from their class. Toby was the only one not in some kind of costume. The others knew not to ask; he had never worn a costume. When they saw Paula dressed in her thrown-together female vampire costume, they joyfully congratulated her on it. For the first time in her life she felt a strong sense of belonging and acceptance. She finally fit in.

The group walked around, growing in number until finally it was time to head out of town and to the barn and the party. To avoid raising suspicion, the large group split into smaller groups and headed in different directions. There were enough younger teenagers still on the streets for the older ones to disappear without being noticed.

3

They stood in front of the candle and said a quiet prayer. They had done the same thing each and every Halloween for the past nineteen years. In other households in town, couples lit a candle before placing carved pumpkins out on the doorsteps with the others that their sons and daughters had carved. They then returned to the front rooms, sat down and read passages from the bible.

Baron had been off school the last two days. He had been advised to avoid others due to him having been diagnosed with a virus. He moaned and argued with his parents about not being allowed out for Halloween. They had stood firm—doctor's orders. Staying in enabled him to see the strange behavior of his parents. They began by lighting a single candle, saying prayers and then carving a pumpkin. He noticed that they had begun to act very strange. As long as he could remember, his mother had always been the stronger, more outspoken of the two, but tonight she was very quiet. His father moved around the house and checked each and every window and locked all the doors. When they sat down and began to read, Baron asked why they had lit the candle and locked all the doors and windows.

His mother spoke quietly; this in itself made him feel uneasy.

'We light the candle because it represents all that is good on this, the darkest of nights. It helps ward off any evil spirits.'

Baron looked at them in disbelief, grunted and headed up to his bedroom, slamming the door just to make them aware of his unhappiness of not being allowed out.

He sat on his bed and stared at the window—doctor's orders or not, he was seventeen and wanted to go to the party. He grabbed his leather jacket and slowly opened the window. He moved through it slowly so as not to make a sound. Once out on the sloping roof above the front door, he turned and slid the window shut. He climbed down the wooden supports of the porch and slipped out into the night.

Paula, Toby and the four others that they walked with had decided to cut through the old church yard. 'It's Halloween after all,' one of them said. They moved amongst the old gravestones, Toby trying his hardest to avoid stepping on any grave. Paula followed his path.

She too didn't want to disrespect the dead by stepping on their graves. The others didn't care; they danced around the headstones, making ghostly calls as they moved. Once clear of the church graveyard, they walked along the deserted, unlit road that headed out of town towards the farm. Whenever they saw a set of car headlights, they ducked down behind the overgrown tall grass that lined the side of the road. When all was clear, they once again continued their journey towards the old deserted farm and the party.

Two groups had reached the barn and had begun to organize the drinks and food onto the small tables that they found in the old house and some that they had made from planks of old wood resting on bricks.

James and Frank stood outside looking at the old tree in the distance. It was there that they would go and use the Ouija board. They walked out, shining their flashlights down at the ground in front of them. The last thing they wanted to do was shine it too far ahead, just in case someone saw the light and came to investigate. They walked down a down a dirt path that was surrounded on both sides by old dying corn crops. Though they were dying, they still stood over six feet tall. They were no longer bright green but brown and yellow. For some reason they had not been harvested. A light breeze blew towards them, making the crops rustle gently. Initially, the sound of the crops moving made the two feel nervous. The light wind would head towards them; they could hear it getting closer as the crops ahead of them rustled and, like a wave got closer, the sound of the dead and dry corn leaves getting louder.

When they reached the old tree, they found that it was surrounded by a circular clearing. There was not even any sign of grass or weed; nothing sprouted from the earth. It was empty and lifeless apart from the tree.

They stared up at the dark shape that loomed over them. The gentle breeze that flowed amongst the smallest branches gave it a sense of life. Branches reached out over them like arms, the smaller twigs looking like and moving like fingers. They looked at each other and smiled. This was a great place to do the Ouija board session, especially if this was the tree that the young girl had hanged herself from. They began drawing a large pentagram in the dry bare soil with their shoes. Once done, they then quickly returned to the barn, chatting excitedly as they went.

4

The group that Paula and Toby had been walking with bumped into another group that was making its way to the farm. They merged as they left the road and began crossing a large field. The further they got from the road the louder they chatted. Toby walked on his own at the back. He was the only one not dressed up. He followed just behind Paula, who was chatting excitedly with two other girls. For the first time, she was accepted and happy to chat with others without the fear of being ridiculed for what she was wearing. She looked back at Toby several times as they moved through the tall grass of the field. She smiled at him and he smiled back. His mind was still back in the garden of the empty house.

They reached the farm and the old barn. The old wooden barn walls allowed green and blue light to escape its cracks as the two lights pulsed in time to the muffled music. The leader of the group pulled on the barn door. The music grew louder and clearer, and the lights burst from the opening and illuminated the group in green and blue. Paula couldn't control her excitement. She grabbed Toby by the hand and pulled him towards the door. Once inside, she paused, her eyes wide, taking in the flashing lights and the group of monsters and vampires dancing in the center. She squeezed Toby's hand tighter as she took in the sights and sounds of her first party. No one seemed to care about how the music sounded tinny; they were all here to have a good time.

Maisey, one of Paula's classmates walked over to her and handed her a large plastic cup.

'Here, drink up,' she said to Paula, touching her cup with the one she held in her other hand.

Paula looked at the dark-colored cup. The flashing green and blue lights made it difficult to make out the actual color of the cup. She raised the cup up to her nose and sniffed. It wasn't the nicest smell she had ever experienced, but she had experienced it before. She took a large sip. The cold liquid that flowed down her throat had a strange taste. It seemed to match the smell, one that was hard to place. She grew up watching her father come home drunk, smelling of what she was now holding. She had seen him sit and drink while watching the Sunday game on TV and always wondered what he was drinking that made him act funny. He hadn't had a drink for three years, well not that she had seen him, but then again, his demeanor was a happier one. She took another mouthful of the liquid. As it moved through her body, it made her shiver.

She handed the cup to Toby, who looked at it and then at the others in the barn who were drinking from the same kind of cups. He took it from her and, in an attempt to impress her, drank it all down quickly as if a can of soda. The taste didn't register until he had dropped the cup empty to his side. The aftertaste made him shiver and screw his face up in disgust. Paula watched with wide eyes and then giggled when he reacted to its taste. She then grabbed him and kissed him passionately before pulling him over to one of the makeshift tables that held the plastic cups full of liquid. She picked up two and handed Toby one. Together they then walked over to where the others were gathered, dancing, and began to move, both a little conscious of how they have never danced in front of others before and worried how they looked to others. After a couple of uneasy songs and finishing off their drink, they began to lose their inhibitions and melted into the crowd, dancing away.

The crowd of alcohol-fuelled teenagers danced happily until the first fight broke out. Two boys from the football team began to push each other on the dance floor. Initially it was fun, but then one shoved the other too hard and he fell to the floor. He returned to the other, who stood laughing, and swung a wild punch. They rolled on the floor trying to hit each other until three of the older students pulled them apart. For some, the evening had been ruined, and they didn't want to be part of any incidents and decided to leave. Toby had seen the two boys rolling on the floor and pulled Paula out of the way. The alcohol in his system had begun to make him feel funny. Paula too had begun to feel the effects of the alcohol. She felt disorientated but happy and excitable at the same time.

Frank took the opportunity while the two drunk fighting friends were being dealt with to stop the music and address the crowd.

'For all of those that want to ultimate Halloween experience, James and I will be conducting an Ouija board session. We have done some research into the area and have found that a young girl hung herself not far from here. Everyone is welcome to join us and see if we can communicate with the other side,' he announced.

There were a few shouts of excitement and a few shouts of, 'Boring get the music back on.'

As he walked over to James, who stood by the door, a group began to follow him. Paula had grabbed Toby's hand and asked if they should go. He had been told of the dangers of playing with anything that can communicate with the dead, but he was feeling strong. He was beginning to enjoy himself and wanted to prove to Paula that he was a man.

'Let's go and see what happens,' he said, pulling Paula with him over to the door and the small group of people waiting by it.

5

The group followed James and Frank down the narrow dirt path towards the tree. The alcohol-fuelled teens chattered away and shone their flashlights in all directions. They no longer cared about being seen. The rustling dead corn leaves made some of the group feel uneasy. Shining their lights at the wall of brown leaves, the shadows cast by the moving leaves against the shaking lights made several question whether there was someone in the cornfield.

When they reached the clearing and the tree, the group spread out, amazed by the sudden emptiness and the size of the tree. They walked around the outside of the marked-out pentagram. Frank and James walked to the center of it and placed the Ouija board on the floor. They called the others to gather round and use their flashlights to help illuminate it.

After a few attempts at scaring the others with forced movements to say various people's names from the group, they asked if there was any young girl present who had killed herself. Frank looked at James and winked. The glass pointer began to slide across to yes, directed by

Frank. It stopped suddenly and seemed to vibrate. Frank's face changed, and he looked at his friend, who looked at him with the same 'Is that you' look. They both let go at the same time and then gasped, as did all that were watching.

The glass pointer began to move slowly away from yes and settled over the no. Everyone sat back and watched the pointer carefully for any more movement, but it didn't move. Frank moved closer and picked up the pointer and looked at it closely. He then lowered his hand down to the board. He felt the cold breeze brush against his hand and smiled.

'It was the wind,' he said with a sense of relief.

The group once again moved closer and chattered with nervous relief. Frank placed the pointer back on the board and asked another question.

'Can you show yourself to us?'

Members of the group giggled and then looked around themselves with their flashlights. Nothing, there was no sign of anything, and then they heard a faint scrapping sound as the pointer began to move once more.

'It's alright, it's only the wind,' one of the group said as others began to back away again.

They watched as the pointer stopped over the letter 'B.' It then moved again, not in a straight line but following the arc of letters written out in alphabetical order.

It paused briefly on 'L' before moving to the 'O.' it again paused and then dropped below the letters, only to return to the 'O.' The pointer then moved its way back along the letters and stopped over the 'D.'

'Blood?' Frank said, confused. The fear of something making the pointer move was lost to fascination and intrigue. Even some of the others who had backed away had returned to watch the pointer move on its own. Paula and Toby were two of the group who had initially pushed themselves away from the board the moment it moved but had returned, fascinated by what was happening.

'Does anyone want to provide the blood?' Frank asked, half joking and half being serious. He wanted to know what would happen.

There was a lot of shaking of heads when he asked for a volunteer. So he asked a further question.

'Why do you need blood?'

The pointer began to move. This time it shifted around the board quicker. Two of the group quickly stood and began to walk away; what was happening, whether a trick pulled by the two who had organized it, was too much.

James spelled out what was being pointed out. This time there was more than a single word.

'We... have... been... told... that... we... cannot... leave... until... blood... has... been... shed,' James said.

'We?' Frank said, looking up at his friend, who shrugged his shoulders.

There was a low thud and then a muffled series of bangs. Everyone looked up at the dark field from where the sounds had begun to grow from. The pointer on the board began to move again.

'She... wants... revenge,' Frank said as he followed the pointer.

'What?' one of the group asked. 'We? She? Who is this?'

The pointer flew from the board and hit James above the eye. He fell backwards holding his face, and everyone jumped back. Those who were standing began jogging away. Those who had been sitting stood quickly. James removed his hands and looked down at them. He could see a dark liquid covering his hands. Frank shone his flash light at him and gasped.

'Holy shit!'

'Is it bad?' James asked, covering his head again with his hand.

A couple of the others came over to him and looked at him, concern and worry evident in their voices.

A stream of blood escaped the barrier that his hand had made and ran down his nose. It pooled at the end until finally, with the gathering mass of liquid aided by gravity, it fell from the fleshy surface of James's nose and fell to the dark earth.

The moment the droplet made contact with the floor, the dead corn field began to sing with a low buzzing sound as a strong wind began to flow through it. Even those who had begun to head back to the barn stopped as the noise grew louder. The thudding and banging sounds increased in number and were joined by distant shouts and screams.

The group beneath the tree began to look around themselves. The noises seemed to be surrounding them. The wind picked up some of the dry dirt at their feet and drove it into their faces. They protected their faces with their hands, trying hard to see from beneath their shielding, saluting-style hands. There was a scream as one of the girls pointed to the darkness of the tree's canopy.

'Oh my God!' she shouted after the scream had died.

The others looked to where her finger pointed. When the others managed to squint through the swirling dirt, they could see a woman in white hanging from one of the thicker branched arms. She was then gone; she disappeared in front of them.

Paula and Toby had both seen the woman and immediately began to run back towards the barn. Others ran past them. Some fell over, the alcohol in their system making running in a straight line difficult. Even the adrenalin rush from fear didn't help as they fell into each other. Those trying to get back to their feet became barriers for others to fall over. At one point there were four people lying on top of each other, each trying desperately to get to their feet. Those who had already made it to the dirt road that led back to the barn suddenly froze as a dense fog burst from the corn field on either side of them, colliding like two waves down the center of the dirt road. Shadows moved within the fog, and voices filled the air. The bangs and thudding sounds echoed around them. They were joined by shouts and screams.

The fog flowed out and across the barren earth that surrounded the tree. James got to his feet and stood with Frank. The two others who had come to his aid moved closer to the two organizers. They all turned back to back as shadows began to move around them from within the fog.

Toby looked down at his feet, trying to see if he could see the dirt road. He was sure he could get back to the barn if he followed it. He strained his eyes, but the flashlight he held just caused a white smoky glare. When he turned it off, he still couldn't see his feet.

'Come on, let's try and get back,' he said to Paula, gripping her hand tighter.

The group that had fallen over each other in their attempt to get away from the woman and the tree stood motionless, their breathing heavy and quick. The noises that echoed around them got closer until a dark shape began to get closer. They expected to see one of the others who had been with them. They all screamed and began running when the figure emerged from the fog. A skeletal face peered at them from beneath a small grey cap. It moaned as its jaw dropped open, and it raised a bony hand towards them.

The four scared and drunk teenagers ran into the field of dead crops. Two of them ran straight into one of the tall dry stalks and fell to the floor. In their panic, they rolled over onto their backs and began crab walking along the floor, looking back towards where they had come from.

Paula gripped Toby's arm. The sudden heavy rustle of leaves coming from the cornfield made her hair stand up on the back of her neck. The sensation of electricity ran down her spine and into her anus as fear gripped her even tighter. Toby began walking slowly in the direction he believed to be the way back to the barn but stopped the moment a large dark shadow began moving towards him. Out if the dense fog, two of the people who had left earlier ran into him and Paula, knocking them over. The two who had just run into them fell too but scrambled quickly to their feet and kept moving. Toby lay on his back. He still held Paula's hand, who moaned and groaned next to him. He sat up and saw several shadows move past them. The fog that hid them swirled, and for a brief moment, a gap revealed a torn pair of trousers surrounding a bony foot. He held his breath and froze before slowly moving to Paula and getting close enough to see her bloody face; her nose was flowing freely. Even in the cloudy darkness Toby could see its wetness on her face. She could feel the metallic taste of the blood and began to panic. Aware that whatever had walked past them may hear her cries, he quickly covered her mouth. Her eyes widened in terror, not knowing why her boyfriend was holding her head and covering her mouth.

'Shhh,' he hissed, looking around him at the dense wall of fog.

One of the girls who had run into the cornfield ran down the narrow dirt path that ran between the crops. She had been lucky enough to avoid running into one of the tough stalks, but the dry dead leaves scratched at her face. She looked back over her shoulder and into the dark swirling fog and then tripped on something. She fell forward. Her scream was brief as it was suddenly turned into a gasping as she fell, unable to judge the distance to the floor. Her outstretched arms reacted poorly and she found the hardness of the ground attacking her chest. All the air in her lungs exploded from her all at once. She struggled to get air into her lungs and instinctively rolled over, where the pressure on her body was less and it was easier to take in the oxygen she required. She opened her eyes wide as she attempted to breathe. A dark shape loomed over her. The fog hid its upper body, but she could see the baggy torn trousers flapping against the thin legs of the person standing over her. Just as she managed to get a lung full of air into her body she saw the long, thin object appear from the fog and enter into her chest. She felt the hollow barrel of the musket enter her. A cracking sound followed as the object was moved back and forth, creating a large cavity that oozed with a dark liquid. Initially, she could feel nothing apart from the sucking and tugging of the gun barrel in her chest, but then it grew, getting bigger and bigger. The pain engulfed her senses, yet she could not let out a scream. There was no air in her lungs for her to use. The musket barrel was pulled sharply from its bloody hole. It hovered over her, and her blood dripped from it and back into the hole it had come from. The last sight her eyes saw was the skeletal face of her attacker as it looked at her during her last moments.

There were screams from the corn field as another student ran into two of the skeletal soldiers who stalked the field. He had fallen, his face sliding along the dirt. Small stones tore at his flesh and buried themselves within the wound. He pushed himself to his knees and raised his hands, pleading with the two skeletal figures. He saw something move through the air and heard the swooshing sound as it travelled towards him. He then felt whatever was moving through the air hit his wrist, it felt like he had been hit by a stick, the dull thud of the impact knocking his right hand down to his side. When he returned it to its original position in front of him. His eyes widened and his mouth dropped open with an almost winded breathless sound escaping. He knelt at the feet of the two dead soldiers, staring at a bloody stump that was once his hand. Blood squirted from the stump where his hand should have been. One of the soldiers stood with a saber. Blood covered its old rusty blade. His skeletal jaw made him look like he was smiling a toothy smile. The other soldier then pushed the barrel of a musket into the eye of the boy and pulled the trigger. The muffled bang and puff of light as the hammer ignited the powder on the side of musket stock illuminated the two skeletal soldiers briefly. The young teenager's body fell forward into the dirt, the back of his head gone. A dark black hole remained of what was once well-groomed hair. The dead corn stalks that surrounded them were now covered in bits of fragmented bone, brain matter and blood.

6

Those that had stayed in the barn and had continued to dance to the tinny sounding music carried on, unable to hear the screams of those outside. One of the older students stood surrounded by younger girls. He enjoyed being the center of attention. The girls tried their hardest to impress him, each one in turn trying to get his attention by outdoing the others with their experience and stories. He laughed at each one in turn, stroking the hair and touching each girl in turn, just to keep their attention on him. He smiled at one of the girls and then something caught his attention—something behind them over by the barn wall. He moved his head and peered past the girls, who in turn looked behind them trying to see what had taken his attention from them.

A grey fog had begun to seep through the cracks and holes of the old barn wall. It flowed through and began to reach out across the floor. The boy looked at it and swore that a strange blue glow was pulsing within it. He looked over to the door and noticed the fog squeeze through the gaps between the door and its frame.

Others in the barn stopped dancing and looked down at the sea of fog as it engulfed the floor around them. Some of the students were too drunk to notice and continued to dance like marionettes, kicking up the fog, making it swirl and lift.

The student who was in charge of the music searched the dimly-lit barn and then noticed a strange figure standing in the center. The long, dark hair and clothing told him that it was a woman. She stood motionless in the center. The fog pulsed with a strange blue color at her feet. Her head moved slowly, turning left and then right. She stared at the youngsters around her.

She had waited for a long time to be freed from the dark and lonely place she had been trapped, her spirit full of hate and vengeance, unwilling to move on. Tonight she had been freed and she was going to make those that killed her pay.

One of the drunken teenagers who continued to dance, oblivious to the fog, was within reach of the strange woman. She reached out and grabbed his sweaty shoulder length hair. He immediately stopped dancing and swatted at the hand that held his hair. The woman grinned at him as his partly limp body moved beneath her grip. The DJ watched, his eyes wide as he saw the woman raise her free hand and then bring it across the face of the dancer in a slapping motion. The body of the boy collapsed into the fog at her feet.

She began to move towards a group of girls who stood around the single male student. The fog that hung around her mid-thigh made it look like she was gliding towards the group.

A couple of others continued to dance and moved towards the center, pumping their fists in the air and jumping up and down. All of a sudden one of them disappeared into the fog. His head reappeared, a look of shock and confusion etched on his face. He could feel something underneath him. He reached his hand up to the others, who helped him up. One of them gasped and pointed to his right arm. The shirt he was wearing had a dark-colored stain on it. He touched it and rubbed the thick liquid between his forefinger and thumb. He then reached down and grabbed the thing at his feet that he had fallen over. He could feel the material in his hands. He pulled, and a wrist and hand appeared out of the fog. The small group gasped and he let go, his eyes wide.

'Who's that?' one of the girls asked.

The boy shrugged his shoulder.

'Do you think he's alright?' another of the girls asked.

The boy looked at his friend and motioned to help pick up the person on the floor. His friend paused momentarily and looked at the fog and then his friend before moving. They reached into the fog and fumbled around for the armpits of the person below them. When found, they hooked their arms under and pulled. The person's chest came up first. Both were expecting to see a limp drunk looking face. They both withdrew the arms quickly and stumbled back away from it the moment both had seen the dark, wet, torn flesh of the boy's throat area. The two girls looked at their dates with wide fear-engulfed eyes as they clung to each other.

The DJ saw the boy's reaction and jumped down from his elevated position. He ran over to where he thought the body was but was looking too far ahead. He caught his foot against the heavy lifeless sack of flesh and fell over the body below the fog. He scrambled along the floor, feeling for it. When he touched it, he pulled at it. When he saw the dark open wound and lifeless eyes of the boy, he dropped the body back into the fog.

The group of girls continued in their attempt to get the older boys attention. He was still looking past them at the woman who slowly approached. The girls didn't notice her presence, even when she stood right behind them. The boy stared at her, trying to see the face underneath the dark, un-kept hair that hung like curtains over her face and down the front of her white dress. He strained his eyes in the gloom, fixated by the woman. The other girls saw his attention was somewhere else and one by one paused. Before they could look around at where he was looking, the woman had wrapped her hands around the nearest girl's throat and began to squeeze. None of the group could move. The boy stared blankly at the woman, as if hypnotized. The other girls could only look wide eyed as the girl being choked gasped for air.

The girl's gasping soon turned to a wheeze as the woman's grip tightened. Her eyes, once wide, began to roll back, revealing an ever-increasing whiteness.

The boy suddenly woke from the trance that had kept him staring. He lunged past the terrified girls and grabbed the woman's hands. He immediately noticed their coldness and bony texture. No matter how much he pulled, he could not loosen the woman's grip. Finally, the young girl gave in and slumped. The woman let her grip go and the girl disappeared into the fog that surrounded them. The group of girls managed to catch their breath and in unison screamed.

Others in the barn stopped their drunken dancing or chat and stared at the group. A few initially laughed but then the high-pitched, terror-infested scream began to eat at their happiness. These screams were different; they were not attention seeking, joking screams. These screams sent shock waves through their bodies. It chilled their bones; it caused the hair on the back of their necks to stand up.

They all saw the woman in white. She stood out amongst the group, her white dress reflecting the strange glow that pulsed within the fog. She flickered, momentarily vanishing from view before reappearing. The boy who had tried to save the girl blinked and stepped back. He couldn't quite believe what he had just seen. She flickered once more and then she was gone. Those that had seen her vanish suddenly found the need to leave. The screaming group of girls began pushing and clawing at each other as they tried to get to the barn door.

There were some in the barn that were still lost in their own alcoholic and drug-fuelled world and continued dancing. The music had stopped; the disc that had been playing reached its end. Even this didn't stop them bopping their bodies rhythmically in time to a tune that played only in their heads.

The woman reappeared in front of the barn door, and several of the teenagers slid to a halt. The moisture that had built up from the fog on the straw-covered wood made it slick. A few ran into those that had stopped and pushed them forward. A blonde-haired boy dressed in a skeleton all-in-one Lycra suit fell and landed at the woman's feet, his white-painted face coming to rest against her cold bony shins. He took a deep breath in and was overcome by a strong, sickening smell. He pushed himself up, quickly appearing out of the fog, coughing and retching as he did.

The woman looked down at him, tilted her head from side to side and smiled. She reached down and put her hands on either side of his head. She then began pushing her fingers into his skull. He grabbed at her hands and tried to stop the fingers probing deeper into his skull. The fingers continued to push deeper, and the sound of his skull giving way filled his head. He didn't feel the pain, just the pop as the fingers pushed past the bone barrier and began pushing into the soft tissue of the brain below. She then curled her fingers around the bone and pulled sharply.

The others who had stopped their advancement to the door watched on in horror as the woman pulled sharply up. The boy's skull separated from the rest of his head. The sudden injection of pain and fear forced his heart to buckle and cease to beat. Blood sprayed those who were at the front. Screams filled the fog-filled barn as girls and some of the younger teenagers reacted to the horror they had just witnessed. Two of the older boys decided it would be easier to rush her at the same time. They agreed while watching their friend being killed that she surely couldn't take on two of them at the same time. They ran forward and tucked their heads into their shoulder as they prepared to shoulder barge her. Just as they were about to hit her, she vanished. Their momentum kept them going until they hit the solid wall of wood of the barn. They missed the door, which would have possibly given way, allowing them to escape. Instead, they bounced backwards and into the fog. They both got to their feet quickly and came face to face with the woman, who grabbed their throats and began to squeeze. They looked at her with wide eyes and tried to pull her fingers from their throats. She just continued to smile at them, her eyes black like polished marbles.

Others had begun to look for an alternative way out of the barn and had noticed the small group pulling at part of the barn wall where the fog was seeping through. They ran over to them and began pulling and clawing at the wooden beams.

The fog continued to flow through the gap in the wall. One of the boys who had joined the original four suddenly let out a gasp and froze. The others looked at him in alarm and stopped pulling at the wooden wall. The boy looked down and saw a large dark object slowly slide from his chest. The others saw the object begin to retract from the boy and slowly backed away from the wall. Once the pointed object had left the chest of the boy and disappeared back behind the wall, the boy slowly turned to them, his hands covering a dark stain on his white sheet he had used to dress himself as a ghost. He looked at them through tear-filled eyes before collapsing into the fog.

The others looked at each other and then at the wall just as several pointed objects began jabbing through the gaps in the barn wall.

***

The woman squeezed tighter and tighter until she felt the two boys' bodies go limp and then let them go. Their bodies fell into the depths of the swirling pulsing light of the fog. She then looked at the group of remaining teenagers who had stood frozen with fear. She sniffed the stale air and moved her head like a snake tasting the air around it. She suddenly stopped. She had found what she was looking for. She vanished once more and reappeared amongst the group that had watched her kill the three boys. The sudden appearance shocked them from their trance and they all scattered in different directions.

One of the girls ran towards where the DJ had stood, elevated above everyone else. As she ran, she tripped over the body that lay in the middle of what was the dance floor. She picked herself up quickly and continued her run to the elevated area above the fog. She focused on the wooden table stacked on the old dry hay bail until the woman in white appeared in front of her and caught her by the throat. The girl's legs shot forward and hit the woman, who held her tight and didn't flinch or move even after the collision. The girl squirmed, and tears flowed freely down her face.

The woman looked at her carefully and then smiled. The girls head became filled with voices. A young child like voice asked if she was one, and a reply came from a much older female voice.

'Yes, she is one of them.'

The girl shook her head, hoping to shake the voices out, but the female voice spoke to her.

'You are one of them. I can sense it in you. Your mother will pay for what she did to me.'

The woman then pushed her little finger into the girl's stomach. It melted the clothing that covered the girl. She could feel the finger pushing against her skin. It was cold, yet it burned. The finger sank deep into her and then began moving slowly down. The clothing that she wore melted away as the finger travelled down her stomach.

The girl gasped as the pain attacked her senses. She could not scream; nothing came out of her mouth. All she could do was take in short bursts of air. Her eyes became glazed by tears that flowed like a waterfall.

The finger was withdrawn and the woman let go of the girl, who stood motionless, still gasping for air. Her hands naturally moved to her stomach and felt the warm wetness of the fluid that was draining from her body. She too then collapsed into the fog.

7

Outside in the fog-filled field, teenagers wandered around, jumping every time they heard a scream, gunshot sound or clash of steel. A small number had stayed with Frank and James near the Ouija board. The tree that towered over them began to creak as a cold breeze flowed around them and the finger-like branches above them.

There was a scraping sound, and the fog began to recede. It moved back to the edge of the clearing and stopped. Like a wall, it surrounded them. The sound that they could hear was the Ouija board glass pointer. It was on the move again, darting from letter to letter. The group approached it carefully, looking down at it and back at the wall of fog.

'What's it saying?' one of the girls asked.

Frank looked at it and tried to make sense of its darting movements between the letters.

'I'm not sure; it doesn't make sense,' he replied.

'What do you mean?' the girl's boyfriend asked angrily.

Frank looked at the girl's boyfriend and then at James.

'It's repeating the same message, or messages. It's almost like there are several people trying to speak at the same time.'

'For fucks sake, what are they saying?' the boyfriend snapped.

James grabbed him by his shirt and glared at him from underneath his bloody compress.

'Leave no survivors. Find and punish the guilty. Let us rest. Cursed earth,' Frank said.

James looked at him.

'It keeps repeating itself,' Frank added.

The girl screamed and pointed at the wall of fog. The others looked to where she was pointing, straining their eyes against the darkness and the fog. Flashes of blue light pulsed from within it, and dark shadows moved around within the thick fog bank. Occasionally a musket barrel or sword tip poked out of it and into the clearing.

'What's going on?' the girl stuttered.

Frank and James looked at each other. Fear filled their eyes and they had no answer.

The scraping of the Ouija pointer suddenly stopped, and an eerie silence caught their attention. They slowly returned their gaze to the board on the floor.

There was a sound of someone stepping on gravel followed by several more heavy footsteps. The group looked up and saw five skeletal figures standing in front of them. The fog no longer hid them. Their clothes were torn and dirty and were old civil war uniforms. They held muskets with bayonets fitted; their empty eye sockets seemed to glow with the same blue that pulsed within the fog.

The group backed away. Frank looked around; the fog still surrounded them like a wall. He looked up at the tree and then shouted to them to climb the tree. They turned and ran the short distance to the tree. Frank helped the girl up to the first branch that was too high for them to reach by standing. When she had moved herself further up the tree via the ever-increasing number of branches, Frank took a step back, used the distance to step in and up onto the tree trunk, using the extra height to push himself high enough to reach the branch. He hauled himself up and then held his hand out for James to reach up. Once their hands were securely linked, Frank pulled James up until he could pull himself up and into the safety of the tree.

The soldiers moved forward, their muskets lowered, the points of the bayonets ready to be embedded into flesh.

The girl's boyfriend looked back. He could feel the fear and panic increase as the soldiers got closer. Frank held out his hand. The initial linking of hands failed, the thick film of nervous sweat causing them to lose grip of each other. The boyfriend jumped up again, desperation in his jump causing him to misjudge the hand being held out to him. Once again he fell. He quickly got himself ready for another attempt, but it was too late. Five bayonets plunged into his back. Frank looked down in horror at the look of terror in the boy's eyes and then watched from above as the soldiers continued to stab the lifeless body.

The girl screamed and then began climbing down from her position high in the tree. Hysteria had overtaken her; she had only one desire and need, and that was to get to her boyfriend. Frank saw her climbing down towards him and grabbed her and pinned her to the thick tree trunk. He tried to calm her by talking into her ear as she fought against him. He closed his eyes tight. He was scared and didn't know what to do, but at that moment in time he didn't want to see another person die.

The soldiers finally stopped stabbing the now squelching body at their feet and backed away from the tree. They looked up at the three students cowering amongst its branches, their skeletal faces grinning as they looked at them. They then turned and returned to the wall of fog and slowly disappeared back into its swirling pulsing depths.

Out on a branch, a piece of old worn rope laid wrapped around it. The tree had continued its growth and the rope had become part of its growing process, embedding itself in the bark of the branch, overgrown with moss and weather-beaten. The rope began to move; it moved like a snake unknotting itself and sliding along the branch. It began to grow in length as it moved.

8

The woman in white stood and looked around the room at the panicking teenagers who scattered themselves around the barn. Some clawed at the walls where they found small holes, others hid themselves behind bales of hay and other objects that lay around the old barn. Her evil smile suddenly changed. Something had caught her attention. Her head tilted from side to side and then the smile returned. She flickered and then disappeared.

The group who had been pulling at the gap in the wall moved together; they stayed close to each other. One of the girls who had been watching the woman in white throughout became aware that she was nowhere to be seen and had not been seen for several minutes.

'She's gone,' she shouted.

Others in the small group looked at her and then around the room. This was their chance to escape. They all ran towards the barn door. Others in the barn saw the sudden movement of the group and immediately joined them.

They pulled at the door, their hands grabbing a space on its edge, and yanked at it. The door moved a little. Soon the group had a rhythm going. The door warped with every push and pull until finally it gave way. It shot open, and those pulling at it fell backwards onto the floor.

Even with the door open, no one moved. They stood frozen to the spot staring at the wall of fog that pulsed with a strange blue light.

The fog had stopped entering the barn; it just hung as if being held back by a piece of glass.

One of the older boys of the escaping group, moved towards the wall of fog and pushed his hand into it. He expected his hand to touch something solid but it disappeared into the swirling fog. He could feel the difference in temperature as soon as his hand entered it, the sharp coldness biting at his skin. He withdrew it and looked at it. He then looked back at the scared crowd of teenagers and shrugged his shoulders. Before he could say anything, he disappeared into the fog, pulled by some force that yanked him off his feet. There were screams from the girls and shouts of panic from the boys, but all had tears of fear running down their faces.

'Shut the door,' one of the older boys shouted before running over to it and straining to close it. Whatever force had held it shut was now trying to keep it open. He was joined by the boy who had been the center of attention to the group of girls, and together they managed to close it, sliding the wooden lock across to secure it. They both leaned against the door in relief.

They breathed heavily, their chests rising and falling in unison, and then the older of the two, who had been the first to try and close the door, gasped. His chest continued to rise. The other boy watched wide eyed as a bayonet appeared from his chest, the blade covered in thick liquid. The blade disappeared and then quickly burst from his chest again. The other boy pushed away from the door and joined the others who watched in horror as the boy slid down the door. A trail of blood marked his descent into the fog that still hung around their legs.

Frank felt the girl slump and stop fighting. He let her go and helped her back up into the safety of the tree. She sat, head bowed and eyes closed. Even with them closed they still couldn't stop the tears from flowing. Frank then moved over to where James sat and began trying to figure out what was going on and how they could stop it.

The rope continued its snaking movement towards the girl until it finally reached her. Like a cobra rising up, ready to strike, it too rose up and watched the sobbing young girl.

The woman in white appeared out on the branch where the rope had begun its journey. She smiled at the girl and blinked her black eyes. The rope shot forward and wrapped itself around her throat. It then pulled her back along the branch until finally she fell. The rope snapped tight, snapping her neck as she swung beneath the branch.

The two boys heard the struggle and watched helplessly as the girl fell.

The woman in white flickered and disappeared, reappearing in front of the hanging body of the girl. The woman seemed to be hovering in mid-air, her hair and white dress flowing around her as if she were under water. She pushed her hand into the girl's stomach, the popping sound of her flesh giving way to the probing hand echoing around the tree. She then pulled at the intestines that began to unravel as they left her body. The woman in white looked over at the two boys and was gone.

Frank and James sat, unable to speak. They both looked at the girl, who continued to swing back and forth by the rope around her neck, her intestines hanging from the open wound all the way to the ground below.

A scream awoke them from their trance. They looked over at the wall of fog and saw Paula and Toby.

Toby had grabbed Paula and dragged her with him, trying to get away from the shadows and skeletal soldiers that moved within the fog. They had burst free of the fog only to find themselves back at the tree where they had started, only this time they were greeted by a girl hanging with her intestines hanging from her. Toby pulled Paula into his chest to avoid her seeing too much of the girl hanging there. He noticed the two boys cowering in the tree. He wasn't sure if they had done this or were victims of whatever was going on.

Frank waved at the couple and called to them to get off the ground and up into the tree. He tried to hold back on making too much sound, fearing he would bring attention to their location.

'Please get up here; they are everywhere.'

Toby paused and looked at the wall of fog and then at the tree. He then began guiding Paula towards the tree trunk, making sure he was shielding her from seeing the girl.

Frank and James moved down to where they could offer a hand and pulled Paula up into the tree with them. They then helped Toby up. They sat on the opposite side of the tree from the hanging girl and discussed what was happening and if they could stop it.

'Obviously the Ouija board was the key to starting this,' Toby said sharply. 'You opened up a door, so you need to close it.'

James held his injured head and shook it. 'We thought it would be fun; we don't believe in this stuff.'

'We did a bit of research, but the first bit of the message was us trying to scare everyone,' Frank said.

Toby looked at Paula, who sat clutching her knees to her chest. He reached over to her and stroked her leg gently. She looked up at him through tear-filled eyes and smiled.

'What history?' he asked.

'This whole area was a civil war battleground; thousands died here,' Frank began. 'I guess we woke them?'

Toby looked at the two boys. 'So who is the woman?'

James looked at Frank and answered with what information he knew.

'She was found hanging from this tree by five of her school friends. The newspaper reports said that she had fallen out with her boyfriend who left town just before she was found hanging here.'

There was a cold breeze that moved through the tree, making the branches creak. Out on the branch that the girl hung from, the woman reappeared.

Paula suddenly sat up and began speaking—but not in her own voice.

'The truth, the truth they hide the truth.'

All three of the boys turned and looked at her with wide eyes.

'Paula, what are you talking about?' Toby asked.

'They stood and watched,' she growled.

Paula then began to shake. Her eyes rolled back, revealing only the whites of her eyes.

'She's having a seizure!' Frank said.

Paula suddenly stood up, her eyes still white over and her body shaking.

Toby stood up on the thick branch he was sat on with the two others and went to grab her before she fell, but he was too late. She shot from the branch she was standing on and out amongst the smaller branches. They scratched at her already bloody face as she moved through them like a rag doll. She came to a stop next to the girl who continued to sway gently from her noose. Paula hung in the air, her head bowed and motionless.

The three boys quickly moved to the other side of the tree where they could see her. Toby felt an electric shock run through his body the moment he saw Paula floating mid-air with the woman in white floating opposite her. Frank and James froze, their eyes fixed on the woman.

Toby quickly climbed down from the tree and ran over to where Paula floated. He jumped up and grabbed at her legs, hoping to pull her down from whatever was holding her there but he just ended up swinging back and forth from her. He let go and turned his attention to the woman. He jumped at her and grabbed her legs. The moment he touched her, he was knocked flying by an invisible force. He landed heavily in the dark dirt below him, all the air in his lungs escaping. He choked as his lungs tried to fill once more, the now dusty air making him cough.

The woman looked at Paula, her eyes widening as the evil smile grew on her face. She raised her hand to Paula's stomach and began to push into her. The woman suddenly stopped, flickered and then disappeared. Paula fell to the ground, her legs buckling underneath her as she collapsed into herself on the floor. Toby rolled and then crawled the small distance to her and hugged her, his tears joining the blood and cuts of her face. She remained unconscious.

9

A set of car headlights approached the barn and the thick wall of fog that surrounded it. Its driver had done the same journey every year for the past six years, ever since Maggie Jackson had been appointed sheriff. She would always drive up and leave a single flower by the tree out in the field.

She had never encountered fog like this before. It seemed to start at the entrance to the field. It had a strange blue glow to it, and in places she swore she had seen dark shapes moving as she drove up the track. She put her fog lamps on, but the reflected light from the fog made it difficult to see so she shut them off and leaned forward, straining to see the edge of the dirt track.

There was a loud, high-pitched scraping sound along the passenger side of the police car. She cursed, wondering if she had strayed from the track and driven into the barbed wire fence that separated the track and the field. She stopped the car and stepped out. She turned her flashlight on and shone it into the fog. The beam did little to penetrate the thick wall of smoke.

She walked around to the side of the car and inspected it. She noticed she was nowhere near the edge of the path, yet there was a long deep scratch that started by the headlight all the way along the side of the car to the tail light.

She felt a cold breeze against her neck, almost like someone had breathed on her. She turned and pointed the flashlight back into the fog, moving it side to side but nothing was there. She felt uneasy, like she was being watched. She placed her hand on her side firearm and slowly moved back around the car to the open driver's side door. She sat into the car seat and reached out to pull the door shut, and that's when she heard the screams. She paused, not sure if she was imagining it, but they came again, along with dull thuds and what seemed like muffled gunshots. She pulled hard on the door slamming it shut, put the car into gear and began accelerating. She turned on the police lights and drove purposely ahead. She knew that at the end of the track was a large barn. That is where she always parked her car and walked the last bit to the tree, but the now swirling and bluish pulsing fog masked all trace of the large building.

Sheriff Jackson slowed her approach. She was sure that she was near the barn, but the lack of visual stimulus made the distance she had driven seem longer than she really had. She stopped the car and pressed the button for the door window to lower. As soon as the window left its seal, she could hear the screams of teenagers and muffled gun shots. She grabbed the radio and called in her location.

'Judy are you receiving me?' she said into the CB radio microphone.

There was a moment of silence and then a response.

'Yes Sheriff Jackson, receiving you,' the voice answered.

'Do we have any other reports of fireworks or gunfire out on the farm road area?'

'That's a negative sheriff, although we have had several calls from worried parents about their teenage sons and daughters not being home,' the dispatcher's voice said.

The sheriff leaned forward and peered into the fog once more and then spoke into the radio once again.

'Yeah well, I'm over at the old farm, and it sounds like the so-called missing teenagers are over here, doing what I have no idea.'

'Roger that sheriff, do you need back up?' the voice asked.

'Erm, no. Keep all cars on the streets to stop any vandalism,' Sheriff Jackson replied.

Sheriff Jackson returned the door window back to its original up position and prepared to get out of the car. Something caught her eye in the rear view mirror. She did a double take and gasped. She recognized the face of the dark-haired woman sitting in her back seat. The sheriff fumbled for the door handle, panic and fear causing her to lose grip and then snatch at the handle before finally levering it open. She stumbled out of the car, drawing her gun as she stumbled to the floor, she stood and pointed it at the car; she could still see the woman sitting in the back seat. She moved around to the front of the car, the headlights of the car casting her shadow against the thick wall of fog behind her.

'Do you think this is some kind of joke?' she shouted, her gun shaking in her hands.

'Get the fuck out of the car, now!'

The woman dully obliged by disappearing. The sudden vanishing caused her to gasp and step back. She felt something behind her and froze. She slowly looked over her shoulder, her gun still pointing at the car. When she saw the woman standing behind her, she lurched forward. She spun and landed on the hood of the car. She pointed the gun at the woman and pulled the trigger. In that moment of panic and fear, she was still aware of the strange muffled sound that her gun made as it fired. It was as if she were firing under water. The two bullets she fired hit the woman, but she didn't flinch, she just stood staring with her black eyes and the sinister smile etched across her face. Both bullets had hit her in the body, but no marks were left on the perfect white dress.

Sheriff Jackson continued to lean against the car, and the gun in her hands shook violently. Her eyes were wide and beginning to fill with tears. She couldn't move; fear had rooted her to the spot. She felt heavy—too heavy to move herself. The woman in white moved towards her and then stopped as two skeletal civil war soldiers appeared from the fog. They looked at the woman in the white dress and then at the other leaning against the car. Their jaw bones twitched as they looked back and forth at the two women. One of them raised his musket up to the woman in white and pulled the trigger. She opened her mouth as if to scream but no sound came out. The skeletal figures began to shake, dropping their weapons before beginning to crumble into fine dust that joined the fog around them.

Sheriff Jackson remained frozen against the car throughout the brief spectral exchange. She was so paralyzed by fear she didn't even notice the warm wetness of her leg and trousers as she lost control of her bodily functions and peed herself.

The woman in white then bridged the gap between them and pushed her body against the sheriff's. She sniffed the face of the lawwoman before placing her hands around her throat.

'I'm sorry. I'm so sorry,' Sheriff Jackson whispered.

Her head then began to buzz before a voice, a voice she remembered, filled her head.

'You are one of them; you did this to me.'

The sheriff answered back through a broken emotional voice. 'It was Jenny; I was just there.'

The voice filled her head again.

'You hounded me, you beat me: you are all to blame for what you did.'

The woman in white then began to squeeze the sheriff's throat. She squeezed until she could feel her body becoming limp and then released her grip. Sheriff Jackson began to cough and gasp, trying to get as much oxygen into her lungs as possible.

The woman then placed her open hand against the sheriff's stomach and pushed. The hand disappeared into the sheriff. She moaned as she felt the burning sensation as it drove through her skin and deep into her stomach. Her eyes widened and she looked down to see the arm sticking out of a wound that pulsed with blood. The woman in white closed her hand around the intestines and pulled back. She held the bloody hand and intestines in front of the sheriff so she could see before dropping them to the floor. The sheriff slid down the front of the car, sitting in her own intestines and blood until finally her heart gave in and she slumped sideways to the dirt road.

10

Out in the field, skeletal soldiers continued their battle, trapped in a constant loop of killing and fighting, occasionally finding cowering teenagers and killing them, not able to differentiate them from oppositional spies and runaway soldiers. They did what they had been told to do: leave no survivors.

The teenagers in the barn continued to cower and hide amongst the objects scattered around the old barn. A small group huddled together trying to figure out a way to escape. They had decided their best option was to try and wait it out until daylight. Someone had asked why then and received the classic response.

'Well you don't see ghosts and undead in the daytime.'

Several of the group nodded.

'But what about that woman,' one of the girls asked.

They all looked around the room; they hadn't seen her for some time.

'Let's stay together and keep away from the walls,' one of the boys said confidently.

Just as he said that, the barn door flew open. The wooden lock could no longer hold back the supernatural energy that pushed against it. The fog no longer stood behind its invisible wall; it cascaded into the barn, quickly filling the room. The teenagers screamed and began running around in blind panic, not being helped by the increasing fog and the bodies that lay on the floor tripping them up. Even some of the small group who had huddled together ran away. One girl ran, looking over her shoulder. She ran straight onto the old rusty spikes of a farm machine, the spikes running straight through her, pinning her to the rusted machine.

Deep within the fog, the skeletal soldiers moved around the barn. Screams, moans and muffled gunshots echoed around the fog-filled wooden structure as one after another teenagers succumbed to bayonets and musket shots. The small group that had stayed together in the center of the barn moved in unison. They pushed their backs against each other, watching for any sign of movement in the fog.

They began moving back towards where they believed the open door was, the fog now so dense that it was hard to see more than a few feet in front of them, especially in the poor light cast by the flashing light and the dim spot lights that had been placed around the barn. Two of the group jumped with fright as a dark shadow moved towards them. Out of the fog, the older teenager fell, bumping into them. Behind him, holding his hand, was one of the girls who had spent so long trying to impress him. No one said a word; they all just continued to move in the direction of the door.

When they finally reached the open doorway, finding it made easier by the blast of cold air blowing through it, they pushed and pulled each other through. The fog continued to blanket everything.

The group stayed together and they continued their huddled movement across the dirt tracks. The older teenager broke away from them and dragged his female companion behind him into the fog. He didn't know where he was going, but anywhere was better than in the barn. The girl he held onto gripped his hand tight. He could hear her sniffling as she continued to cry.

The girl suddenly became heavy to pull along, her grip no longer tight but limp. He stopped and looked at her. She stood looking at him with a blank expression. She then fell forward past him and disappeared into the fog below him. He still held her hand. Where she had stood was a skeletal soldier, his toothy grin chattering away as if laughing. Its musket and bayonet that had been plunged into the girl pointed at him, and a dark liquid dripped from its end.

In a fear-fuelled rage, he knocked the musket out of the way and ran his forearm into the soldiers face. The head of the skeletal figure popped off its connective attachment and disappeared into the fog. The body stood motionless, frozen in the same position. The teenager backed away. Tears filled his eyes, his breathing heavy, causing his chest to rise and fall rapidly.

The bayonet then shot forward and into his face. The blade entered through the boy's eye socket and exited through the back of his skull with a crack.

The small group of huddled friends moved through the fog, pausing whenever they heard the sound of a footprint or saw a shadow move within the fog. A faint sound caught the attention of one of the boys, who held out his arms and stopped the group.

'Can you hear that?' he asked, whispering just enough to be heard. His friend looked at him with concern and then listened.

There was a strange crackling sound and then a voice spoke before the crackling sound began again.

They looked at each other, realizing that what they were hearing was a radio CB. They began moving the group towards the crackling static and voice until they saw the two beams of light and then the car itself, although they could only make out the headlights and everything above. The fog seemed to be even thicker below their knees. The driver's side door was open, allowing them to hear the person on the other end call for a response.

'Hey the cops are here,' one of the girls said with an element of relief in her voice.

One of the girls decided to stand in the light. She moved to the front of the car and kicked something at her feet. She looked down and noticed she wasn't touching the car. She kicked out her leg again. Whatever it was it had a strange soft texture to it.

'Mike, can you come here please,' she called.

The boy who had first heard the car radio looked up at her from peering into the car through the open door. He walked over to her and asked what was wrong. She explained that there was something at her feet in front of the car that felt a little strange. He looked down as she told him, unable to see anything. He reached down and put his hand into the thick swirling fog. His hand touched what the girl had been kicking against and could feel some kind of fur. He wrapped his hand around it and pulled. It was heavy, so he grabbed it with his other hand and pulled harder. The face and wide eyes of the sheriff appeared from the thick river of fog. He let go straight away.

The radio crackled again. 'Sheriff come in.'

Mike moved back to the open door and picked up the radio mic, squeezed the side button and spoke into it.

'Hello.'

The voice responded immediately.

'Who is this?'

'My name is Mike Tanner, we need help. Please send help.'

'Ok Mike, where is the sheriff?' the voice on the other end asked.

After a brief pause, he answered. 'She's dead.'

The others in the group who had gathered around the open door all looked at him.

'What do you mean dead?' the voice shouted back.

'She has been killed.' He began to cry.

'By whom?' the voice asked. He could tell the other person was struggling to keep their emotions under control.

'We don't know. We need help,' he said in response.

The voice answered quickly telling him that there were other officers on their way and not to move from the car. The group of teenagers looked around them at the thick fog, the headlights throwing up a wall of light that encased them, the beams of light unable to penetrate the dense wall. One by one they pushed themselves into the safety of the car and shut the doors.=

11

Toby held Paula tight. He didn't care about what was moving around in the fog, the screams or the woman in white. She could appear and try and take Paula, but he was willing to give his life in protecting her.

'Hey, get back up here,' Frank called from the tree.

Toby ignored him.

Paula's eyes flickered and then slowly opened. Toby took a sharp intake of breath. His eyes widened and a smile broke onto his dirty face.

'Oh baby, its ok I'm here,' he said gently.

She looked up at him. For a moment, she stared into his smiling face and then her expression changed to one of horror.

'What? What's wrong?' Toby asked, his smile fading and being replaced by concern.

'She won't stop until she has had her revenge.'

Toby looked at her. 'What do you mean?'

'She showed me what they did to her,' Paula said before beginning to cry.

'Who?' Toby asked sharply.

In between her sobs she answered, the words sending a shiver down his spine.

'Our parents, our parents were the ones who killed her.'

Toby pulled her close and hugged her until he heard the two boys in the tree call to him to move. He looked at them and then in the direction they were pointing.

He looked at the figure standing in the clearing. It wasn't a skeletal soldier or the woman in white but a pale-looking male figure in a leather jacket. He looked harder and recognized Baron. He lived a few houses down from him.

'What the fuck is going on?' he asked aggressively.

'I got lost on the way up here, but have seen some strange shit! Dead people and skeletons walking around and, oh my god who is that?' he said, looking at the disemboweled girl hanging from the tree.

'Get away from the fog,' James called.

Baron looked back at the wall of fog and moved quickly over to Toby and Paula.

As he walked across the dirt, he noticed the Ouija board on the floor, the glass pointer spinning in its center.

'Who brought this over here?' he said, pointing at it.

'Erm, we did,' Frank said sheepishly.

'You dumb shits!' Baron returned. 'You've opened a gateway for all those that have been trapped here to walk on the earth again.'

Toby looked up at Baron and raised an eyebrow. 'What, seriously?'

Baron looked a down at him, 'Think about it, it's Halloween and everyone knows about all the death that happened around here during the civil war.'

'But what about the woman?' Frank asked.

Baron paused and looked at him confused. 'What woman?'

Paula then began talking, telling her the visions that she saw when the woman in white had taken control over her.

12

Tina walked to school on her own every day. She was the outcast. She dressed different to all the others in her class, partly due to the lack of money to buy the latest fashionable clothing and her liking of heavy metal music. She was used to being the new student. This was the fifth school and town she and her mother had moved to in the last twelve months. Her abusive father always seemed to find them, forcing them to leave in the dead of night and run to the next town.

She was stared at constantly, remarks were made endlessly, small groups of girls whispered as she got changed in the changing rooms for phys. ed., comments on her scars and burn marks on her upper thighs from where her father had put his cigarettes out to teach her a lesson.

One group of girls was worse than all the others; the cheerleaders were the cruelest of all the groups, often hiding her clothes or putting them in the shower to get soaked, only to laugh at her and comment on how they needed to be washed.

They had locked her in rooms, barged past her, knocking her books to the floor several times and written notes about her and passed them around classes. She endured the sniggers, finger-pointing and rumors for several weeks.

Even though the other kids didn't like her and school was hard, she was glad that she and her mother had stopped looking over their shoulders after her father had been arrested for assaulting a woman who had refused his advances at a bar some twenty miles away.

One afternoon, she was on the end of another malicious bullying attack by the cheerleaders, being pushed around the corridor as she tried to walk past. Other students stopped and laughed as she was sent crashing to the floor. After the lead cheerleader stuck her leg out and tripped her over. Her books flying everywhere; some were kicked further down the corridor by one of the group who had always been the quieter, less-bullying girl.

The bell rang for the start of the next lesson and the corridor soon became deserted. The gang of girls walked past Tina, who lay on her back looking up at them.

'Don't stay down there, you are making the place look untidy, bitch,' Mandy, the lead cheerleader said, looking down at Tina before moving on with the others who looked at her and laughed.

Tina lay there asking herself what she had done to them to make them treat her like that. She sat up and looked around at her books scattered on the corridor floor. She heard footsteps and turned to see a boy dressed in jeans, a white T-Shirt and denim shirt bend down and pick up two of her books before crouching down next to her.

'Hey, are you ok?' he said softly.

She sat just looking at him. She was prepared for him to say something hurtful or throw the books he had picked up further down the corridor because that's what everyone else in the school would have done. But he didn't, and that amazed her.

'Let me help you,' he said, placing her books in one hand and holding out his free hand. She took it and he pulled her up onto her feet. He then continued to pick her books up. She stood and just watched. This was the nicest thing anyone had ever done. He returned with all her books tucked under his arm.

'I'm sorry about what the girl's did,' he said.

She shyly shrugged her shoulders and bowed her head. She could feel the nervousness building in her stomach.

'What lesson you got now?' he asked.

'Chemistry,' she replied quietly.

'Come on, I'm going to that part of the building. I'll walk you there,' he said.

They walked down the corridor together, the boy introducing himself as Thomas, 'T' to his friends. She told him her name and he smiled.

'I guess I'll call you T as well.'

She smiled, for the first time since arriving in town she felt a sense of happiness.

Over the next few weeks, the girls continued to berate her and bully her. Some of the boys had begun to get into the act until Thomas stopped them. He was, after all, the school star quarterback. He wasn't like the other jocks; he was intelligent and wanted to go on to study medicine.

The girls had seen them together, talking, Tina laughing and flirtingly stoking his arm. Mandy's anger grew within her. She had been trying to get his attention for the last year and believed that being the top cheerleader, she should be the only one that the school quarterback should date. Whenever she tried to flirt or get his attention by cornering him at his locker, he politely smiled and made an excuse before moving on. The other girls in her little gang agreed with her that they should be dating and went out of their way to try and get them alone, with many of the other girls also dating football players.

The grief Tina got from the girls became something she could block out. She began to look forward to coming to school, just to see Thomas. It made all the hurtful things and bullying mean nothing.

Thomas had begun to spend more and more time with Tina, often going over to hers to study together, walking her home if she missed the school bus and even spending Saturdays at the ice cream parlor in town.

They had been seen by a few of the cheerleaders who had told Mandy straight away. Mandy sat at home, jealousy burning within her, her hate for Tina becoming overpowering.

Over the following weeks, things began to change for Tina. The cheerleaders began to ease off her. They even began to smile at her when they saw her in the corridors. She thought that Thomas had said something to them.

In reality, Mandy was conducting her great plan. She was not going to lose the boy she wanted to the new girl; she was going to make Tina pay for taking him away from her.

Life both in and out of school was easier. The cheerleaders seemed to want to get to know her. The pain and fear of going to school had begun to disappear as she finally felt accepted. Her mother had secured a job at an out of town diner; she was finally happy. Tina was also happily in love with Thomas. The friendly hug had soon become a kiss on the cheek and then the romantic film cliché of staring into each other's eyes, smiling at each other as their lips met. This had progressed to fondling each other and then, one Saturday afternoon, while her mother was out, her first sexual experience.

The cheerleaders began slowly including Tina in their conversations when they all got changed for and after phys. ed. lessons.

'What you think Tina?' Mandy asked her as she put her new bra on, cupping her breasts and smiling at her.

Tina looked up from re-lacing her boots and just nodded.

The group of girls looked at each other and smiled.

'Hey Tina, do you have any other clothes that aren't black or grey?' one of the cheerleaders asked.

Tina looked up again and shook her head.

'When's your birthday Tina?' another of the girls asked.

'Next month,' she replied quietly.

'Oh really, when? We should do something,' Mandy said excitedly. The excitement wasn't because of Tina's birthday but for what she had already planned.

Tina looked up at the group of girls, all of whom seemed to be excited and discussing what they should all go and do.

Today was a bad day. She had spent the last few weeks worrying, even to the point that she had called off dates with Thomas, saying she wasn't well.

As her birthday approached, she began to revert to her shy lonely self. Thomas had tried to persuade her to tell him what was wrong, but she kept saying nothing. He spoke to the cheerleaders, warning them to leave her alone, but they just said that they were all friends and planning to go out for her birthday.

He walked her home after one of his football practices, happy that she had decided to stay and watch. They walked, Tina hugging her books close to her chest. He asked what was wrong. She stopped looked up at him and sighed, tears beginning to run down her face.

Mandy had noticed the distance between Tina and Thomas and laughed; they had split up or were not talking. This was her chance. She had her plan in place. Saturday morning she was going to trick Thomas to the old farm and force herself on him. It would be easier now that Tina was out of the picture. Then all the girls were going to take Tina out and build her up with a false sense of security before taking her over to the farm and telling what had happened between her and Thomas. She had even brought a length of rope as a joke that she was going to fashion into a noose and place it around her neck. They were going to make Tina's birthday one she'd never forget. Just thinking about it made Mandy smile more.

Thomas received a letter, slipped through the side of his locker door. He looked at the light blue envelope carefully. He looked around him at the other students who passed him in the corridor or stood in small groups chatting.

He smiled briefly. 'Tina,' he said to himself before moving his head further into his locker and sniffing the envelope. It didn't smell like the perfume that Tina wore: the one he had become used to and the one he identified with her. But he had no reason to think that the envelope he held in his hand was from anyone else. He opened the envelope and unfolded the piece of paper inside. He expected to see Tina's handwriting but was met by a typed letter. He began reading it, occasionally looking behind him to make sure that none of his friends were standing behind him reading it over his shoulder.

Dear sweetest Thomas,

I know things have been difficult recently but I do love you and want to see you this Saturday. You are the only birthday present that I want.

I know you were planning to go out with your friends Saturday night, after all it is Halloween. I would love to see you during the afternoon.

I want to make my special day even more special by spending part of it with you.

Meet me at the old farm on the outskirts of town at 1pm.

Love you.

Tina

xxxxxx

Thomas smiled as her read the letter, since they had last seen each other and she had told him she no longer wanted to see him, he had felt so helpless. He really didn't care about going out with rest of the football team Halloween night. All they ever did was throw toilet paper over the police station and dress up the town's statues. He wanted to spend Saturday with Tina. One thing that played on his mind was the location of the meeting: the old farm. Why not his or her house?

He hadn't seen her for the last few days and worried about her. He had called round, but no one answered. He read the note again before replacing it in the envelope with a smile. He placed it in the back of his locker and paused, looking at it briefly before the bell rang out to signal the need for all students to begin moving to their next lesson.

From down the corridor, the group of cheerleaders huddled together. Each took it in turns to watch his reaction and feedback to Mandy, who stood with her back against the wall. When one had begun reporting what she had seen, another began looking.

Mandy had already shared with the group what she had brought for Tina. She had found an old white dress in a charity shop in town.

'The bitch is cheap and nasty, so she deserves cheap shit clothing,' she said to the others with venom in her voice.

The group of girls had arranged to meet Tina at the ice cream parlor at three Saturday afternoon before moving on to implement the rest of Mandy's plan.

Tina had avoided Thomas. She had not attended school in the last few days because she had been feeling unwell. Her mother had noticed that Thomas, who she had liked, had not been around recently and attested her daughter's illness to her falling out with him.

She sat in her room on her bed and rubbed her stomach, her mind full of questions. She didn't want to tell her mother, she couldn't tell Thomas and her birthday was only two days away and she was meant to be meeting the group of girls she had become friends with. Maybe she could talk to them? But then her head quickly threw that idea away; memories of how they treated her because she was different raced back into her head.

13

Saturday morning Thomas woke excited. Today was the day he got to meet with Tina. He spent longer than normal in the bathroom, causing his mother to knock on the door to see if he was alright.

He had showered, played with his hair, trying different styles. He wanted to make an impression. Today meant the world to him. He sat in his room watching the clock, every second feeling like a minute, every minute an hour, every hour dragging its heels.

He decided to leave early and walk slowly to the farm. He ran through in his head what he wanted to say and at times found that he was talking to himself.

He walked up the dirt path, the chill in the air forcing him to pull his leather jacket tighter and zip it higher. He reached the large old barn. The fields that surrounded him were full of old dead corn. He looked at the brown dead stalks and remembered the stories around town about the field of corn that never tasted right because of all the death that happened in the fields during the civil war.

He stood outside the barn and looked around. He checked his silver Casio digital watch. The grey and black digital display showed 12:56 pm. He then heard a door open. He turned around and saw Mandy standing in the old barn doorway in just her underwear, her white bra and panties standing out against the darkness of the interior of the barn.

'Hey Thomas, glad you came,' she said provocatively.

Thomas stood staring at her, confusion etched on his face.

'What's going on? Where's Tina?' he asked.

The cold air bit into Mandy, her skin mottled with different shades of red, pink, light blue and whites from the cold. It made her skin dimple with goose bumps but she felt only the heat of her excitement.

When he mentioned Tina, anger began to build within her.

'You don't want that cheap weirdo,' she answered back.

Thomas' face began to show more anger. He was angry that he had been fooled.

'Everyone knows that the head cheerleader and the school star football player should be dating,' Mandy said.

'I don't want you! You are everything that I don't like about school sport. Tina is different. She's smart and not false like you,' Thomas said.

The words that he said cut deep into Mandy. The anger that she felt for Tina was now unbearable, and she could feel hate for him. She looked down at herself. Suddenly she felt the cold.

'I've come here to show you that we are meant to be together, I'll give you whatever you want. You can take me now,' Mandy said, her voice showing signs of anger.

Thomas shook his head and turned away. He began walking away. Mandy's eyes widened as he turned his back on her. She looked around and saw a large stone not far from where she was standing. She moved to it picked it up and ran towards Thomas. He didn't hear her approaching but felt a sudden dull impact on the back of his head. His vision wobbled. He tried to refocus but found everything appearing fuzzy. He turned and saw Mandy, her hand was raised above her head. She held something in it but he couldn't make out what it was. She brought the stone down on his head once again. Her anger grew; it never subsided. She continued to hit him across the head even after he had fallen to the floor. She straddled him and pounded the stone into his face. Even the spray of blood and the feel of the warm liquid running down her arms didn't stop her.

When she did finally stop, her heavy breathing clouding in the cold air, his face was a dark, bloody cavernous mess. His legs twitched as his nervous system continued to fire. She dropped the stone and stood, the anger on her face almost becoming an evil grin.

She looked around and walked calmly back to the barn and put on her clothes. She looked around the barn and noticed an old shovel in the dim light. Once dressed, she returned to Thomas and began dragging his body past the barn and into the corn field. She cursed as he got caught against some of the stalks. She cursed more and kicked his body. When exhausted, she stopped and realized she was covered in sweat.

'I offer my body to you and you turn me down, and now you're making me get dirty and sweaty,' she said angrily.

She returned to the barn and grabbed the shovel. She dragged it behind her, its rusted blade chinking as it slid over the rocks in the loose dusty soil.

She dug a hole and dragged his body into it. She looked at his watch to check the time and smiled. She still had time to get back, get changed and meet the others. Her anger was now excitement. She was excited because of the thought of Tina suffering. She felt no remorse for what she had just done; she felt empowered.

Tina walked slowly into town. She didn't want to stay in any longer, but she was also really not up for socializing with the giggling group of girls. She knew if she blew off the girls it would mean going back to them giving her grief, so she was willing to endure the afternoon.

She saw the others sitting next to the window. They were deep in conversation. When they saw her they waved. She smiled and entered. They all moved up so she could get onto the large red single seat that wrapped round the table. They clapped and sang happy birthday, and Mandy handed her a small present wrapped in paper that had jack-o-lanterns on it.

'Sorry about the paper, but it is also Halloween,' Mandy said.

They urged her to open the present, which she did. For that brief moment, she had forgotten about her problems. When she removed the white dress, her secret crashed back to the forefront of her mind.

'What's the matter? Don't you like it?' Mandy asked.

'Er no, it's nice,' Tina responded.

Two of the girls grabbed her hands and pulled her off the seat.

'Come on let's go and try it on,' the one said, wrapping her arm around Tina's.

Tina looked at her with surprise. 'Where?' she asked.

'In the restroom, you got to put it on,' the other said, wrapping her arm around Tina's other arm and walking her into the restroom. They stood and watched as she took off her faded black jeans and Iron Maiden T-shirt and then pulled on the dress.

Back at the table, Mandy recalled to the others how she had seduced Thomas, letting him do whatever he wanted. The other girls asked for details to which Mandy was happy to give.

'He bent me over a hay bale in the old barn and took me from behind. It was so nice,' she said, her imagination creating the images for her, playing them in her mind like a movie.

In the restroom, one of the girls gathered up her clothes and walked out back to the others. The remaining cheerleader helped Tina do up the small zip on the back of the dress and then led her back to the table, where she was met with claps and whistles.

Tina sat down. She had not worn a dress since she was six and felt a little uncomfortable.

They all sat chatting away, the cheerleaders looking at each other, smiling and laughing every now and then. For some unknown reason that bewildered Tina.

Once they had finished the ice creams, the group of girls led Tina out of the parlor and up out of town. Tina had asked where they were going several times and was told not to worry; it was her second present.

They arrived at the dirt road that led up to the old farm. Tina looked at the dead stalks and felt a chill run through her.

'Why are we here?' she asked the group, but they didn't answer.

They walked up to the barn. Mandy made sure she avoided walking near the damp slightly red dirt where she had beaten Thomas earlier.

They walked over to the barn door and Mandy opened it. They walked in one by one, the cheerleaders giggling to each other as they entered.

Tina stepped into the dimly lit space and looked at the group of girls who now stood in a curved line in front of her.

'So?' Tina said, shrugging her shoulders.

Mandy laughed, followed by the other girls.

'Well you see tramp,' Mandy began, 'earlier today, me and your boyfriend met in this very place.'

Tina could feel her heart sink. Her stomach suddenly made her feel sick.

'What you saying?' Tina asked.

'He couldn't keep his hands off me. He made love to me in here,' Mandy continued, enjoying seeing Tina become uncomfortable.

Tina turned and moved towards the open door but felt her hair being yanked back. She reached up and clawed at the hands that had clamped around her hair. She recognized the voice as it cursed. Mandy had grabbed her and was pulling her back deeper into the barn. Tina lost her balance and fell backwards onto her backside; the hands that grabbed her never let go. She found herself being dragged across the floor. When Mandy did let go of Tina's hair, she walked around her as she lay on the floor, giving details of what Thomas had done to her. The other girls gathered around and laughed at her.

The tears poured from her face. She watched as Mandy prowled around. Once she had finished telling her story of her and Thomas, she then began shouting insults at her.

'You think you can come to this town and take the best looking boy from me?' Mandy shouted before bending down and pulling Tina's hair back.

Tina was forced to look into the face of Mandy, who moved in nose to nose with her and shouted at Tina. Mandy let go quickly of Tina's hair, causing her head to fall forward. Mandy slapped Tina hard across the face. The other girls all laughed and began kicking dirt and hay that lay on the barn floor over Tina.

Mandy slapped Tina again and again. Tina's face became red to purple in color. Soon, the dirt-kicking girls began kicking Tina, first in the legs and then in her back. Each time Tina tried to crawl away from the attacking crowd, she was yanked back by the hair.

Mandy moved past the group of kicking girls and walked over to a bag that had been sitting on an old wooden crate. She reached behind it and pulled out a length of rope and returned to Tina.

One of the girls saw Mandy with the rope and stopped the kicking.

'What are you doing?' she asked Mandy.

Mandy looked at the smaller blonde cheerleader and sneered at her.

'You are either with us or against us. If you want to join the bitch on the floor then fine,' Mandy snapped.

The young girl looked at Mandy, shock and fear etched on her face. She didn't want to be on the wrong side of Mandy and the others.

Mandy pulled the noose over Tina and pulled the rope tight. The other girls stopped their onslaught. Mandy then began dragging Tina back towards the door. Some of the girls laughed and began barking.

'That's it bitch, go for a walk,' one of the others shouted.

Mandy dragged Tina along the floor until she finally managed to get to her feet and relieve some of the pressure from the rope. Mandy continued to pull Tina out of the barn and down a small dirt road surrounded by the dead corn until they reached a large tree. Tina fell to the floor again, coughing and gasping for air. Mandy looked at the other girls and smiled.

'I'm going to make sure she gets the message. You lot start heading back; I will catch you up,' Mandy said.

The other girls nodded and began walking away.

Mandy turned her attention back on Tina. She grabbed the rope and threw the one end over a large overhanging branch. She threw it over again and then began to pull. The rope tightened again around Tina's throat. Mandy could feel the excitement of watching her suffer and soon she was winching Tina off the floor. Tina's legs began kicking thin air as she struggled against the rope. She could feel her life ebbing away.

Mandy pulled again on the rope and Tina's body jerked higher. Mandy watched until Tina had stopped kicking and then let go. Tina began falling to the floor, but the rope suddenly snagged on a small protrusion on the branch it was wrapped around. Tina's descent to the floor jerked to a halt, and her legs collapsed below her. Mandy looked at her body, limp and swaying gently, Tina's legs acting like an anchor. She walked over to Tina, knelt down and whispered into her ear.

'Thomas never did anything. He didn't want me. He wanted you, you dirty bitch, so I killed him because if I can't have him no one will.'

Those were the last words that Tina heard before her life ended.

Mandy ran and caught up with the others. She ran towards them shouting.

'She's killed herself. She's killed herself.'

The others stopped and looked at Mandy,

'She became crazy and hung herself, I tried to stop her but she climbed the tree, wrapped the rope around a branch and jumped.' Mandy said with tears running down her face.

The group of girls ran back up the path to the tree and saw Tina hanging, her legs limp underneath her.

'Oh my god what do we do?' one of the girls shouted.

Mandy looked at all the girls and began to explain what they should all say. If they told the same story then they would never be accused.

They nodded and began their journey back to town. When they came across a phone booth, they called the police, who met them up at the farm. They stood by the barn and gave their statements, each one identical. They had come over as a Halloween dare after celebrating their friend's birthday in town, Tina had recently been dumped by her boyfriend who had left town.

The town's sheriff and his deputy's looked around and found nothing else. The story that the girls had given seemed rock solid. It was an unfortunate love-sick suicide. They looked into Tina's and her Mothers past when they delivered the news to her mother. She blamed herself, especially when the autopsy found she was pregnant. The local newspaper ran the story of a heartbroken teenage girl, pregnant and abandoned by her boyfriend, committing suicide.

When the other girls read the article and saw that Tina was pregnant, all but one felt sick and guilty. Mandy just smiled, when she was asked about when she saw Thomas last, she just kept up the pretense of having sex with him that morning and that was the last she saw of him.

Tina's body was taken back to where she was born and buried next to her grandparents. Her mother never returned to the town.

The cheerleaders never left town. They dated and married other local boys and football players, becoming well to do stay at home mothers, all except one who chased a dream of becoming a police officer. When she did, she worked her way up the ladder until finally she became the town sheriff. Even though she knew what punishment and cruelty she and the others had done to Tina all those years ago, she was still afraid of Mandy.

They met regularly, Mandy organizing drinks and evenings together. She bossed her husband around something rotten. Some of the others couldn't believe how she treated him. She kept her daughter under a tight leash. They all attended church on Sundays with Mandy being one of the church leaders. It was the power she liked; being part of the church gave her certain powers over the townsfolk. She was well known for reciting scripture and verse freely when she needed to control a situation. The others attended church, some not really wanting, to but that was also an order from Mandy.

A few of the other ex-cheerleaders lit a candle each year in memory of a girl who committed suicide on her birthday. All but Mandy felt the guilt of that day. The sheriff still drove over each Halloween and placed flowers by the tree.

14

Mandy had ordered her husband to call the police and tell them that their daughter had not returned home. When he put the phone down and told his wife that the officer had said that several others had also called worried about their sons and daughters whereabouts and that she was sure that they were all fine and to call again in an hour if she had not turned up, Mandy released a torrent of abuse at him. She picked up the phone and called the police station. Her husband sat down quietly and listened to her shout at the person on the other end.

'I don't care about anybody else's sons or daughters, I want mine found and brought back home now. You get on the radio and tell the sheriff that Mandy wants her to find her daughter,' she shouted down the phone before slamming it down.

She stood by the window and stared out into the dark streets, the street lamps illuminating small areas along the sidewalk. The much larger trees cast darker shadows, reducing the lamps' effectiveness.

She heard a siren break the calmness of the night and then saw the red and blue flashing bounce from house front to house front as the car approached and then sped past, followed by another. Mandy could feel something was not right. There was something eating at her; this wasn't normal. She ordered her husband to get in the car. She placed the key in the ignition, pulled the gear stick into drive and then slammed her foot down on the accelerator. The car shot off the drive and turned sharply to follow the two police cars disappearing in the distance. Her husband sat in the passenger seat gripping the handle above the door with both hands, his knuckles white with pressure as he held on. He looked at his wife's face. Her expression of anger told him not to speak. He had seen this look several times before, and when he had tried to speak to her, she had become so angry she had attacked him, punching him in the face, on occasions leaving him with a black eye.

Baron's parents heard the screeching of tires and sirens and watched as the two police cars drove past. They looked at each other and then heard another car, its engine screaming from the acceleration. They watched as Mandy's car flew past.

Baron's mother looked over her shoulder at the single candle burning on the mantelpiece. She gasped as it suddenly went out. She ran to the stairs, her husband close behind. She reached Baron's room and barged the door open. She fumbled along the wall for the light switch. When the light came on and she saw the room was empty, she screamed.

Her husband managed to catch her as she collapsed. He pulled her to their bedroom and placed her up onto the bed. She lay in a fetal position, crying hysterically. He left her and ran down the stairs, grabbing the car keys that hung on the hook by the side of the front door and began unlocking it. Once free from the numerous locks, which his wife had insisted on he, pulled open the door and ran to the car. He yanked the door open and dropped into the seat. He then pushed the key into the ignition and quickly turned the key and held it there until the old Volvo started. He reversed at speed off the drive, the tires screeching as he hit the brakes, put the car into drive and accelerated off in pursuit of the other cars.

He was in such a rush and panic he didn't even notice he was driving with no headlights on.

All four of the cars raced out of town and towards the old farm.

The teenagers hiding in the police car lay motionless. Even those who were being sat on had no desire to try and move to be in a more comfortable position. They jumped whenever they saw a shadow move past the car. Even the girls who had been crying uncontrollably had managed to stop, or at least had stopped the sounds of their crying; tears still flowed down their cheeks.

Mike Tanner lifted the radio to his mouth and quietly spoke into it.

'This is Mike Tanner, are the others on the way?

The radio was silent for a few seconds and then the voice on the other end replied, breaking the eerie silence of the car so much that the others began telling it to shush. Mike pulled the mic into his chest to muffle the sound.

'Officers are on the way. Do not move from your present location.'

There was a clanging sound and then a sharp, high-pitched screech as a bayonet was dragged along the side of the police car, followed by another on the other side. The occupants of the car fidgeted nervously and then the windows exploded in. Skeletal hands grabbed at the youngsters, who kicked out at them trying to beat them away.

One by one they were pulled from the car until only one was left. Mike pushed himself into the foot well of the passenger seat. The others continued to fight their bony abductors, their screams filling the cold night air. They were dragged deep into the swirling fog. The skeletal soldiers took it in turns to run their bayonets into the teenagers they had dragged from the car. Two of the girls found themselves looking into each other's eyes as several rusty bayonets plunged into their backs. Their wide eyes looked deep into the other as their life escaped them. One of the boys kicked out at the hand that held onto his ankle. He felt the floor change from rocky to leaf filled dirt; he realized he was being dragged into the corn fields and kicked harder. The soldier stopped, looked down at the kicking leg and raised his free arm. The saber he held in his hand came down and sank into the bone of the boys shin. He screamed, feeling the dull thud and then searing pain in his leg. The soldier raised the weapon again and hacked down again and again until the ankle he held came away from the rest of the leg. The soldier then walked to the boy's upper body and hacked at his head until it split in half diagonally from his left temple to the right side of his chin. Other screams filled the air until suddenly they stopped. All that was left was the thuds and bangs of gunfire.

Mike remained curled up, staring at the seat in front of him, his breathing more of a gasp.

15

Baron looked at Toby and then the two boys still sitting in the tree. Paula had finished telling them the visions that had filled her head, placed there by the woman when she had taken control over her.

'So what do we do?' Toby asked Baron.

Baron shrugged his shoulders and then looked back at the Ouija board and its pointer that continued to spin in the center.

'The board is the key. If we destroy the board then maybe that will close the gateway,' Baron said.

Frank and James looked at each other and nodded. They then looked back down at the three students below them and out at the board.

'Who's going to get it?' Frank asked nervously. He wasn't going to volunteer.

Baron looked at Toby and Paula and then up at the other two in the tree.

'I will help Toby get Paula up on her feet and support her,' he began. 'Who has a lighter?' he then asked.

Frank felt his heart sink; he knew he had the lighter in his pocket.

'I do,' he said disappointedly.

James began moving down the tree until he was able to hang low enough from a branch to drop down to the soil below. He looked at Frank and waved him down. Frank sighed and began moving himself onto the same branch that James had used to hang from. He lowered himself until he was hanging and then let go. He misjudged the distance and ended landing on the side of his right foot. His body weight forced his ankle to buckle and roll underneath him. Amongst the dull thuds and bangs of gun fire echoing around them, the sound of his groan as he tore the ligaments of his ankle made the others all look over at him. He collapsed in a heap on the dusty floor, clutching his ankle. He rolled back and forth, cursing between gasping for air and moans of pain.

'Can you not do anything right?' Baron said.

James bent down, his head still throbbing. Bending down to his friend added to the pressure and dull ache. He put his arm under Frank's armpit and hauled him up onto his one leg. He leaned against his friend, hopped a few times and wiped away the tears that had filled his eyes.

'You wait by the tree. I will go get the board,' James said to Frank, who nodded and hopped over to the tree trunk and leaned against it.

Baron watched as James slowly walked towards the Ouija board. He quickly looked away when he felt Paula become heavy and collapse. Still holding onto her, he and Toby dragged her over to the tree, where Frank stood, and sat her against the trunk.

James looked at the wall of fog, his slow walk stuttering each time he saw a shadow glide past within it. He reached the board and its spinning glass pointer and crouched down to pick it up. He didn't take his eyes off the wall of fog until he realized he was feeling around in the dirt and not feeling the board. He quickly looked down and grabbed the edges. He didn't want to touch the spinning pointer and picked up the board, keeping it flat, allowing the pointer to continue its spinning motion. He turned and began his slow walk back towards the tree and the others. He no longer cared about the fog; his attention was firmly fixed on the spinning glass pointer.

He managed to get within twenty feet of the tree and his friends when a dull thud sounded behind him. He felt like someone had poked him with a finger in the back, the sensation made him raise his eyebrows and look up from the board and at his friends. His legs suddenly buckled and he began to fall forward, a sudden searing pain raced from where he had felt the strange sensation on his back to his eyes. As he fell, he threw the board forward. The glass pointer never left the board as it flew several feet forward; it continued its spinning motion.

James fell heavily into the dirt, his arms slowing him down enough to stop his face crashing into the earth.

Frank saw his friend fall and for a moment all his pain had gone. He pushed away from the tree and steeped towards his friend but fell to the floor, pain filling his head as his swollen injured ankle gave way and he fell to the floor. He looked up from where he lay and saw a skeletal soldier walk from the wall of fog and towards James.

The soldier walked up to the injured boy, his back covered with a dark moist stain, grabbed his ankle and began dragging him back towards the fog. James could do nothing. He could not feel his legs and he was losing his strength to try and pull away from his abductor. He looked at his friends, tears filling his eyes as he was finally pulled into the wall of blue-tinged fog.

Frank lay in the dirt, tears streaming from his fear-filled wide eyes. Baron looked at Toby and then left them and ran to the Ouija board that lay on the floor, its pointer still spinning. He brought it back to where they sat under the tree, placed it down on the dirt and then helped Frank back up.

'Where's the lighter?' He asked.

Frank fumbled around in his pockets, not sure which one he had put it in. He reached into a small inside breast pocket and pulled it out. Baron snatched it from his hand, flipped the silver hood off the flint and lighter part and thumbed down hard on the circular part that caused the flint to spark. The flame jumped into life. Baron held it there for a second and looked at the Ouija board on the ground.

'We need something to help it catch alight,' he said, releasing his thumb from the lighter, extinguishing the flame.

Frank looked at him and then at Toby, who looked up from kissing Paula's forehead.

They both shrugged their shoulders. Baron then looked down at his T-shirt and began tearing off a section from where the seam began. He pulled the material until he had a long length of T-Shirt hanging from his hand. He reignited the lighter and held it under the dangling material, it began to burn with growing yellow flames. He then draped the burning material on to the board.

The flames flickered in the small breeze that swirled around them, the board began to darken where the flames ate into the surface. They watched as the Ouija board began to catch fire on the corner. The board hissed as it began to burn. Frank looked up at the wall of fog, hoping to see it disappear now that the board was burning, but it continued to swirl and pulse with the strange blue hue.

16

The police cars skidded into the dirt road of the farm. The officers stared wide eyed at the wall of fog ahead of them. They slowed their approach and put on the side searchlight, hoping to pick out anything that may be hidden within the dense swirling fog. The rear police car suddenly jerked forward, the officer being thrown forward. His seat belt snapping tight. He stopped the car and radioed to his colleague in front that he had just been hit by something and that he was going to check it out. The radio crackled and then a voice responded.

'Ten four, you need back up?'

The officer looked in is rear view mirror and could see the bright spots of light from another car.

'Just don't go anywhere; looks like someone has driven into me,' he answered.

The lead police car stopped, its brake lights casting a red glow in the thick smoky fog that surrounded it.

The police officer who had been hit grabbed his flashlight from the passenger seat and pushed the door open. He walked, gun drawn and the flashlight held over the wrist of his pistol carrying hand towards the headlights of the car that had hit him.

When he arrived at the driver's side door, he called for the driver to step out slowly. The door didn't move. The window made a whirring noise as it began to lower. The officer moved back slightly and pushed his gun out further towards the driver's side door.

'I said, step out of the car,' he said more assertively.

The door still didn't open but the window finished its descent.

'Why have you stopped?' a voice barked.

For a split second he was stunned. Who had spoken to him like that? Then he recognized the voice as it continued to shout at him from inside the car.

'Why have you stopped? We need to find my daughter!'

The officer lowered his gun and approached the open window.

'Listen, you shouldn't be here. You need to go back home,' he said.

'Don't you dare tell me what to do. I supported you in getting your job, now I want you to do what I pay you for and that's find my daughter,' Mandy barked.

The officer looked at her angry twisted face and then saw her husband sat in the passenger seat, staring straight ahead.

The window then began its journey back up before he could even say another word. He had felt the rage of the woman once before when someone had hit her car. All the evidence suggested she was at fault. When he suggested that she was, he found himself being reprimanded by the sheriff for accusing the woman of being in the wrong and lying about what had happened. She had so much power in the town that no one dared cross her.

He returned to his car and radioed to the other officer in front.

'I'm ok, but we got company. The wicked witch of the west just ran into my car. She's looking for her daughter.'

The radio buzzed and then a reply came.

'Oh shit, that's all we need.'

The officer took his foot off the brake and continued his slow drive along the dirt road until he reached the sheriff's car.

He radioed to the officer behind that he had just found the car and that it had its windows smashed. The other officer stopped when he saw the red lights of the car in front and then got out and joined his fellow officer who stood, gun drawn behind the driver door.

Mandy saw the brake lights and quickly stopped. She shut the engine off and got out quickly, running forward until she was standing behind the two officers.

'Ma'am you need to get back in your car. Please go back and stay with your husband,' the officer told her.

Again she angrily stared at him and told him that she wanted them to find her daughter and she had every right to be there to make sure they did their job correctly.

Mandy's husband sat in the car. He didn't want to step outside into the strange fog but knew if he didn't join his wife he would pay the consequences later. He pushed his door open and walked to where he could hear his wife's voice. When he arrived by the car, he could see she was berating the police officers, pointing her finger at them and then out in front. He could hear her demanding that they go find her daughter. He drew level with her. The officer who was taking the verbal abuse saw him.

'Sir, could you please take your wife back to the safety of your car?' the officer asked.

Mandy's husband sighed and put his hand on her shoulder and quietly told her to come back to the car. She turned and looked at him, her anger boiling over.

He tried again to get her to go back to the car with him by putting his arm around her and trying to guide her back with him. She snarled at him and then punched him in the face. His nose exploded with a popping and thudding sound. He fell backwards and disappeared into the thick fog. The police officers stood stunned; they couldn't believe what they had just seen. Groans came from within the fog and then Mandy's husband reappeared. He stood and looked at them through tear-filled eyes, blood smeared all over his face. He turned and walked away, disappearing back into the fog.

'What the,' one of the officers said, still shocked at what had just happened.

Mandy looked at the two officers and snarled. Her clenched fist waved at them.

'You boys had better find my daughter or else you'll never get another job in this town or state again once you've been fired from this one for incompetence.'

They looked at each other and knew that she had the connections and power in the town to make life difficult for them.

The two officers walked slowly towards the sheriff's car. They each took a side and began inspecting the interior through the broken windows, their torch beams crossing as they both shone into the rear seats. They moved further along. The officer on the driver's side peered in and could see nothing. The other officer shone his torch in through the passenger window and saw something move in the foot well. His immediate reaction was to step back and raise his gun. His partner saw him react and also took evasive action, backing away from the car with gun drawn.

The officer on the passenger side took a deep breath and stepped towards the door. He held the flashlight between his shoulder and ear and gingerly, keeping his gun pointing at the cars open window, reached forward and pulled on the handle. The moment the door began to swing open he grabbed the flashlight from its temporary support and shone it at whatever he saw move in the foot well.

He saw the tear-smeared face of a boy, his eyes staring lifeless at the seat. The officer motioned to his colleague, who moved quickly around the front of the car, ready to assist him. He managed to get to the hood of the car and then tripped over something. He fell forward, disappearing into the thick fog that surrounded their feet. He sat up and looked back but could see nothing. He reached his hand into the swirling dense fog and grabbed what felt like hair. He pulled at the object, raising it enough for it to appear out of the fog. The deathly stare of the sheriff caused him to let go of the hand full of hair.

'Jesus,' he shouted, crab-walking away.

The other officer who was quietly talking to the traumatized boy looked up when he heard his partner shout. All he saw was the faint outline of the police officer's head bobbing up and down as he moved away from the car.

'What's wrong?' he asked.

'I found the sheriff,' he said in between large gasps of air.

Mandy had heard the commotion and ran towards where the officer was talking to the boy. She pushed him aside and looked into the car.

'Paula?' she asked.

When she realized that it was not her daughter, she groaned angrily and walked off into the fog in search of her daughter, cursing as she went. The officer who she had pushed past watched as she disappeared. The other officer, who was back on his feet, also watched as she marched past him.

The boy stayed firmly wedged in the foot well of the car. The only movement he made was the constant shaking of his body and quivering of his lips. The officer tried once more to get the boy's attention but realized that whatever had happened was so traumatic that he was in no state to be moved. He removed his radio from his belt and spoke into it. The other officer joined him, looked into the car at the boy and then shone his torch into the fog. He was sure he had seen something move within it.

'This is Officer Walker, up at the farm, we need paramedics and forensics up here right away,' he said before pausing. 'Better wake the county medical examiner as well.'

The voice on the other end responded, the usual calm voice was now broken and emotional.

'Copy that, we are getting calls about missing teenagers. What's going on up there?'

The officers looked at each other and shrugged their shoulders, neither wanted to venture any further.

'We don't know. We've located the boy; something is not right up here,' he responded.

Mandy's husband stood by the passenger side door of their car. He wiped his blooded, tear-filled face with his T-Shirt. He had accepted numerous beatings at the hands of his wife throughout the years, blaming himself for her anger and pain. He had stopped loving her years ago. He had thought about walking out on several occasions, but not only did he fear that if he left he would never see his daughter again; he was sure she would kill him.

He stood against the car and wept. He then heard the sound of a car approaching, its engine screaming.

Baron's father had lost sight of the other cars and had driven past the dirt road to the farm. When he could not see the police cars' flashing lights or the taillights of the other car in the distance on the straight road, he pushed hard on the brakes; the car skidded to a halt. He turned the car around and headed back the way he came. As he drove back along the road, he searched the dark fields for any sign of where the cars had gone. He looked out at the fields and noticed a wall of fog. He stopped the car and looked at it, amazed that it seemed to be trapped within the confines of the barbed wire of the boundary of the field.

He began moving slowly down the road until he came to the dirt road that led into the fog. It was then he saw a strange pulse of blue. He hit the brakes and looked into the fog. A second pulse of blue appeared and then another and another. His brain shouted to him that it must be the police cars and pushed hard on the accelerator pedal. He was a man obsessed. He still had no headlights on and was speeding up as he travelled up the dirt road. The fact that he couldn't see what was in front of him didn't matter. His son was all that mattered.

He didn't see the other car until he hit it. The car ploughed into the rear of the stationary car. Baron's father gasped as his car launched into the air and began to rotate. The car managed a complete three hundred and sixty degree roll before cashing back to earth. The connection between the front of the car and the corn field soil acted like a massive brake, the force of the impact throwing Baron's father into the windshield. His head exploded as it was forced against the glass barrier, the impact causing the windscreen to become a blooded spider's web of cracks.

Mandy's Husband saw only a glimpse of the car as it hit, its rising trajectory causing the front bumper to hit the side of his head just below his ear, decapitating him.

The officers heard the explosion of sound coming from behind them and automatically ducked. The officer who had stumbled over the sheriff's body was hit in the chest by an object, knocking him backwards back beneath the thickest blanket of fog. Whatever it was had come to rest in his arms as they instinctively wrapped themselves around whatever had hit him. He sat up and looked at what he was holding. He screamed when he saw the head of the Mandy's husband. He threw it to the side and stood up quickly. He could feel the wetness of the head's blood on his jacket as he brushed his hands on his front trying to get any remnants of the head off him. They heard the sound of the car land but did not see it.

17

The Ouija board began to burn with a green flame, Frank gasping as it did. Baron however, didn't seem bothered by the bright, odd-colored flame.

'Don't get too excited; the color of the flame is probably because of the chemicals used on it,' he said confidently.

The board began to warp under the heat; it began to bubble and then spit, launching small embers through the air and landing on the dirt floor. The glass pointer continued its crazy spin in its center.

Frank looked up from the board and gasped, the cold night air flooding his lungs. He moved back towards the tree, his eyes wide and fixed on something ahead of him. Baron looked at him and then in the direction he was looking. Standing on the edge of the clearing stood the woman in the white dress.

Toby looked at Frank and then to the woman.

'Shit,' he exclaimed.

The woman flickered and then disappeared. Baron moved slowly towards Toby and Paula.

'Is that the mystery woman?' he said as he got closer to Toby.

Before he could answer, the woman reappeared, standing in front of Baron. He felt the lightning bolt of shock and fear shoot through his spine.

The woman stared at him with lifeless black eyes and an evil grin etched on her face. She flickered again and he found that when she stopped flickering in and out of his vision, she had her hand around his throat. He could feel her bony cold grip beginning to tighten. He tried to pry her hands away but found her strength unearthly.

The Ouija board continued to burn just behind the woman, the flames growing larger and brighter. There was a bright flash that caused all of them except the woman to blink, followed by a strong blast of air.

The wall of fog pulsed quicker and quicker, the blue light becoming a rapid beat. The fog itself began to slowly lower until finally it exploded up into the air. It momentarily hung and then began to fall back to earth as a blue-tinged fine rain.

The soft thuds and bangs of gunfire ceased, as did the cries and shouts of battle that filled the fields.

***

The police officers began to take a deep breath when the felt and saw the fog that surrounded them begin to pulse and then explode around them. When the fine rain had fallen and settled, revealing the large barn in front of them, they sighed. They looked down at their feet with their flashlights and saw the body of the sheriff and the head of man who had accompanied his wife. They looked at the field where they had heard the car crash to the ground and saw the mangled remains of the car. Smoke and steam rose from its engine.

Mandy had continued her march, not sure where she was going, noticing dark shadows move around her. Each time she saw one, she called her daughter's name. When the fog began to pulse blue and rise around her, she still continued her march. Nothing was going to stop her. When the blue fine rain fell, clearing her ability to see, she found that she was on the old dirt path that led to the large old tree.

***

Frank found a surge of strength. The fog had gone, and he could not see any soldier. The only spectral thing left was the woman. He launched himself at her, ignoring the pain from his ankle.

She flickered as Frank's body got close, and disappeared, his momentum carrying him past Baron, who began gasping and fell down into the dirt. He moaned as he hit the floor.

The woman reappeared in front of Baron, her hand returning to his throat. He began struggling for air once more.

The woman's grip grew tighter and tighter. He could feel the sensation of sleep creeping in; he knew his time was nearly done. The vision of the woman became more and more blurred as he began to lose the fight to live.

He suddenly felt his throat fill with cold air and then his lungs begin to work hard to replace the oxygen they had been starved of. His vision slowly improved, and he noticed she was gone.

'Paula!' Mandy shouted, her voice piercing the night's silence.

She listened carefully and then called again—nothing. She then continued her march up the dirt path towards the old tree.

She called again, but this time she got a response.

'Over here,' a voice whispered.

Mandy stopped and looked around her. The voice continued to repeat itself. Its chilling whisper seemed to be coming from different places. Each time she heard it, she turned quickly to where it had come from.

'Who is that?' she shouted.

'You know,' the voice answered back.

'Show yourself,' Mandy demanded.

She then heard another voice; this voice, however, had a sense of panic to it.

'Up here,' it said, loud and high pitched.

She looked around her once more, seeing nothing. She continued her march up the small incline of the dirt road to where the last voice had come from.

18

The police officers made their way over to the smoking wreckage of the car. The now blood-stained officer shone his flashlight at it. He paused when he saw the bloody mass sticking out of the windshield. The other officer turned away quickly when he caught sight of the man with his flashlight beam.

'What the fuck is going on here?'

The blood-stained officer shrugged his shoulders and began walking back to the car where the boy still cowered.

The red and blue lights of approaching police cars and the larger ambulance made them both sigh with relief.

The cars pulled up, the drivers quickly getting out and joining their colleagues. The EMTs rushed up to them carrying their bags of medical equipment and were pointed to the sheriff's car. The two paramedics looked at the car then the officers and then back to the car before moving quickly to its open doors and the boy.

'What's going on?' one of the new arriving officers asked.

The two original attending officers looked at each other and began to recount what they had seen. As they gave their account, two of the other officers broke away from the conversation and headed over to the old barn. They drew their weapons and slowly stepped through the open door into the darkness of the barn's interior. The beams of light from their flashlights danced around the barn's interior; nothing moved within.

As they moved forward deeper into the darkness, they both caught their feet against something—and then again as they continued moving forward. When they pointed their flashlights to the floor, they both gasped and retreated quickly back to the open door. Once back outside, one of the officers grabbed his radio and began speaking into it, his voice broken and disjointed with panic.

19

Mandy reached the top of the small incline and saw the large old tree. Beneath it she could see a number of people. She increased her pace. When she saw her daughter sitting against the tree with Toby crouched next to her, she broke into a run. She ignored the girl who hung from the tree and the two boys who were kneeling in the dirt trying to help each other, the one coughing as if he had been choked.

She reached her daughter and grabbed Toby by the shoulder of his jacket.

'What have you done to her,' she shouted at him angrily.

Toby stuttered and raised his hands in a defensive pose.

'Nothing, I haven't done anything. It was the woman,' he said.

Mandy snarled at him and then let him go. She then knelt down by her daughter and began to shake her, hoping to wake her from her semi-unconscious state. Paula's eyes fluttered and then opened, her mother's face gradually coming into focus.

'Why did you do it?' were the first words out of her mouth.

Mandy looked at her, confusion stretched across her face.

'Do what?' she replied while stroking her daughter's hair.

'Tina. Why did you do it?' Paula continued.

Mandy stopped stroking her daughter's hair and stood up.

'What you talking about? That bitch killed herself,' Mandy snapped.

Toby looked at Mandy and then at Paula.

'What's she talking about?' he asked.

It was at that point that the two boys who were helping each other shouted in unison.

'She's there.'

Mandy looked behind her and saw the woman in white standing by the body of the young girl who had been hanging from the tree. She stroked the rope that held the girl's body and it began to move. It uncoiled itself from its noose, the body of the girl finally falling to the damp, blood-soaked earth. The intestines that had hung from the opening in her stomach now surrounded her face.

The rope moved back up into the branches of the tree and began to snake its way towards the five people gathered by its large ancient trunk.

Frank looked at Baron. 'Why hasn't she gone?' he asked.

Baron looked at the now charred Ouija board and noticed the glass pointer still spinning.

'The pointer,' he said in response.

Mandy looked at the woman, memories flooding back, as did the anger of that day.

'You slut! You dare try and hurt my daughter,' she shouted and began walking towards her.

Tina flickered and disappeared. Not even seeing her disappear stopped Mandy, her anger so powerful she felt no fear of the spirit that had returned. Mandy walked several steps and then felt something wrap itself around her throat. The rope had snaked its way to a large branch just above where Mandy was standing. It reared up like a cobra about to strike and then launched itself at her. Mandy reached up and pulled at it. The rope began to tighten, causing her to gasp for air amongst her cursing.

Paula screamed. She tried to get to her but collapsed back against the tree. Toby pushed himself up and ran to Mandy, attempting to try and remove the rope as it began to tighten.

Tina flickered into view. She stood in front of Mandy and smiled. Mandy let go of the rope around her throat and swung wildly at Tina, who stood just out of reach. Toby let go of the rope and lunged at the woman. Just like she had done with Frank. Just as he was about to hit her, she vanished, sending him to the floor before reappearing. Toby tried to get back up but found that an invisible force held him down against the dirt.

The rope fell from the tree and began moving its way like a winding snake across the floor towards the dead corn field. Mandy felt the pull of the rope; she tried to fight against it, but it continued its relentless pull. She fell on her back and began to be dragged across the dirt floor. Tina watched as Mandy passed by. She then looked up at the dark figure standing within the boundary of the corn.

Baron watched as Mandy struggled against the snaking rope on her journey towards the corn field. He caught a glimpse of a dark outline of a man standing amongst the dead corn. He then refocused his attention on the Ouija board and the spinning glass pointer and made a move towards it.

This was the key, he was sure of it. If he broke the glass then the doorway that had allowed the woman in white into this world would be broken and she would be sent back. That was the only way she could still be here. He brought his heavy boot down onto the burnt board and the spinning glass pointer. He had a sense of relief when he heard the cracking of the glass below his boot. He ground his foot down, making sure that the glass was crunched into thousands of little pieces and watched the woman in white.

Something was wrong. He pushed on the broken glass harder, but she was still there, walking alongside the woman being pulled by the serpentine rope towards the cornfield.

Paula sat, unable to move against the tree. Tears streamed down her face as she watched her mother disappear into and amongst the corn. Frank sat, mouth open unable to move or speak.

Toby still struggled against the invisible force that held him down in the dirt. Baron stopped twisting his foot into the board, glass and dirt.

20

Mandy struggled, trying to pry the rope away from her throat. It was tight enough to restrict her intake of air and stop her from getting her fingers around it. She occasionally reached out and grabbed an old corn stalk, hoping to stop whatever was pulling her. Tina walked past her and began walking alongside the dark figure.

Tina and the figure walked into a small clearing in the field and paused in its center. The rope continued its journey until Mandy had also reached the small clearing and the feet of the two figures standing in its center.

Mandy lay, staring up at the star-filled night sky, and the tightness of the rope released. Two faces came into sight: one being Tina, whose black eyes and evil smile stared down at her. The other face looking down at her, also with black, lifeless eyes, was that of Thomas. Mandy gasped with fear.

Thomas reached down and picked her up by her hair. For the first time in her life Mandy was frozen with fear. Voices began to fill her head: the voices of her two victims, the voices of the two who were going to exact their revenge this cold Halloween night.

'We've waited so long for you,' Thomas's voice echoed.

'You took my life, my love and my baby,' the second voice screamed.

'You are going to endure pain like you never have,' Thomas's voice added.

Mandy could not move; she was paralyzed. She could do nothing as Thomas dug his fingers into the flesh of her perfect face, his dark pointed nails sliding between her skin and muscle. Tina began pushing her hand into Mandy's stomach. The burning sensation as it penetrated beneath her soft skin caused her to urinate herself. The warm wet sensation as it ran down her leg and soaked her trousers made her feel dirty and worthless.

Thomas began to peel back her skin, strip by strip from her perfectly formed face. She could feel the tearing and pulling as her skin was removed but could do nothing but endure the pain as it flooded her senses.

Tina pushed deeper into Mandy's stomach, wrapping her hand around the soft, silky feeling intestine and then pulling sharply back. Tina enjoying showing Mandy her own intestine in the moonlight.

Thomas pulled the last piece of skin off the left side of Mandy's face. He then stepped back along with Tina. He looked at her as she stood, slightly swaying. They smiled and embraced. A bright light encased them. Its brightness grew and grew until finally it exploded out in all directions. When it faded and the darkness of the night returned, Tina and Thomas were gone.

Mandy collapsed to the dirty floor where her life slowly drained from her. Her blood soaked into the dirt of the clearing and soon her life was gone.

21

More police cars arrived. Word had got out of the strange macabre findings up at the old farm. As the sun began to rise, several officers found four teenagers up by an old tree. The boy would not leave the side of his girlfriend. When they had tried to separate them, he had begun to scream, only stopping when he was allowed to hold his girlfriend's hand. The girl herself was nonresponsive. She was stuck in some form of trance. Incidentally, her father had been killed when a car had crashed into his vehicle in the fog, decapitating him. Another boy had a broken ankle and was speaking gibberish about soldiers and ghosts. A third teenager spoke of gateways and spirits. When he was told his father had died in a car crash not far from where he stood, he had to be sedated after becoming hysterical.

The biggest and strangest scene was in the large old barn, where protruding out of the solid dirt floor, hands reached up. The FBI were called, and after a thorough investigation it was determined that the large number of teenagers that had been found buried in the barn were part of some strange religious cult suicide.

A body of a woman was found in a small clearing in one of the fields. She had been identified as a local power-mongering religious council member. It seemed like she had ripped off half of her own face and somehow managed to disembowel herself. Even stranger was that when they removed her body, they found a shallow grave directly below where she was laying. The bones in the grave suggested that a teenage male had been killed via several blows to his head, based on the damage to the skull.

None of this made it into the national papers or even the local papers. The only reference to the large number of disappearances of teenagers in the town was a bus crash A crash that never happened.

The surviving teenagers were placed into a psychiatric hospital and soon forgotten about and all records of what happened that night disappeared.

Some towns have secrets, some darker than others that must never see the light of the day.

The End.

Other Books by Peter Buckley.

The Burning (Supernatural Tales book one)

The Burning

A band of marauding outlaws leave death and destruction as they travel the plains of the Wild West. Tonight a soldier who fell victim to them while protecting the woman he loved will be resurrected by a Navajo chief, to exact a painful and personal revenge on each of the seven.

Driftwood (Supernatural Tales book two)

Driftwood

Jane Mellows and her daughter Megan had
escaped the city to start a new life in the
picturesque harbour town of New London,
Massachusetts. Out in the dark waters of the bay
an ancient evil stirs. It has risen from the depths,
its blood lust so great that it will stop at nothing
in its quest for revenge against the town that had
tried to destroy it centuries earlier

The Mansion (Supernatural Tales book four)

The Mansion
A team of paranormal investigators spend the
night in one of the most haunted buildings in the
United Kingdom, hoping to capture some proof
of the existence of ghosts and spirits.
Deep within the grounds of Hallstorn Manor the
Spirits are preparing to reveal their existence.

For more information on all titles from Peter Buckley go to:
www.peterbuckley.info where you will find all up to date information and links to amazon and other sites where you can purchase his books.

Follow Peter on twitter @PBuckleyBoH
Also on Instagram pbuckleyhorror

www.ingramcontent.com/pod-product-compliance
Lightning Source LLC
Chambersburg PA
CBHW060428130626
46555CB00005B/2269